Twisted Isla

By

Lynda L. Lock

&

your friend Sparky

Dedication

This book is dedicated to the front-line workers and the people who donated their time, money, and efforts to help their fellow islanders and their pets survive during the COVID19 pandemic on Isla Mujeres. Thank you all!

And as always, in loving memory of my best friend and adventure partner - Lawrie Lock

Chapter 1

January 2nd Nashville Tennessee

Suzanne Hamilton-Forbes flicked her long perfectly-shaped fingernail, snapping it against a brochure for a music festival beginning on February 4th. Her eyes flashed with anger. Her two-timing husband Brandon Forbes was participating again this year. If he thought he could continue to embarrass her with an assortment of over-sexed beach bunnies, he really didn't know her at all.

At thirty-five she was in her prime. She was tall, thin, beautiful, and rich. Very, very rich. Daddy-dear had been obscenely wealthy and he had recently died at the relatively young age of sixty, conveniently leaving her, his only child, a vast fortune. Her mother whom she hadn't seen for twenty years was comfortable with her divorce settlement, but not as wealthy as her only daughter. Fortunately, after their divorce Daddy-dear had never remarried preferring instead to have a never-ending stream of progressively younger blondes to entertain him. There was no one that she had to share her vast inheritance with, it was hers, all hers.

She had everything men fantasized about including her own Phenom 300E jet which she was licenced to fly. Her little French-style Chateau in the upscale neighbourhood of Belle Meade was an average sized house for the area; twenty-five thousand square feet with ten bedrooms, twelve bathrooms, and a recording studio that would have made Kenny Chesney envious. The house was a comfortable size, unlike her drafty castle in northern Scotland, and her sprawling hacienda in southern Spain. Daddy's 197-foot yacht was still berthed in Monte Carlo. It was listed for sale with a broker for somewhere around fifty million dollars, but she would take less. She loathed the yacht, it reminded her of a floating sex-parlor with its six luxurious suites, spa, and massage salon.

That adulterous piece of shit that she was married to had no right to treat her so badly. Brandon had been a dimple-cheeked, blonde, ah-shucks, country boy when they met ten years ago. Despite Daddy-dear's warnings that the man was a penniless swindler he had endeared himself with thoughtful gestures, little gifts, and foot massages.

After their marriage she realized her father was right. The rat was flat broke and only wanted access to her money. Fortunately, her father had insisted on a prenuptial agreement drawn up by the best lawyer in Nashville. Even if she died, her little prince charming wasn't going to get a cent more than an agreed upon allowance. Her assets would be sold off, leaving the bulk of her fortune to an Ivy League university. Her cadre of lawyers had negotiated the deal. She really didn't give a damn about the snotty-nosed entitled students that her donation would benefit, she just wanted her name to be memorialized on a stunningly beautiful edifice.

The easy thing would be to buy off her mate. She could easily set Brandon up with his own recording label and let him chase his ridiculous dream of being a bigtime country star.

No, that wasn't adequate revenge for the social humiliation of his serial infidelities. Perhaps she should anonymously attend the music festival, and perhaps her unfaithful spouse would have an unfortunate accident, or perhaps he should succumb to a severe case of food poisoning. She smiled coldly at her reflection in the full-length mirror.

Yes, that's a much better idea.

Lightly brushing her fingers down her throat and over her large breasts, she imagined the touch of a new and younger lover. Of course, there would have to be a suitable mourning period for her parasitic spouse.

"Alright," she spoke aloud, "enough daydreaming. I need a plan," She sat at her desk and opened the web, searching for accommodations using the incognito-mode which wouldn't leave cookies on her internet history. She wanted something suitable but not too flashy and definitely nowhere near where the Nashville crowd would be staying.

Using a credit card that she had applied for several years ago with the fake name of Sophia Hayden-Smith, she booked two-weeks at a large oceanfront home that was tucked into a secluded neighbourhood. It had eight bathrooms, five king-sized ensuite bedrooms, two kitchens, and a swimming pool. It was suitable.

Included in the weekly rental fee was a private limousine service from the airport to a marina. At the marina she would transfer to their personal yacht and be delivered directly to the dock in front of the home, avoiding the crowds of tourists riding the passenger ferries.

The rental agency offered the option of full-time staff and a shopping service for an additional fee. She clicked yes on the reservation form. A request popped up, asking that she email her food and beverage preferences within the week, so as to give the staff time to find her specified choices.

A two-week rental was more time than she needed, but she wanted to arrive early to do a little reconnaissance work. She also arranged for a golf cart to be delivered to the house on the day of her arrival. It was a charmingly simple mode of transportation that would help her blend in with the islanders.

She closed the laptop and moved outside to the sunny patio just off of her bedroom. Touching an app on her phone she called the kitchen and ordered a glass of sweet tea to be delivered to her.

As she sipped the cool beverage, she planned how to change her appearance. She couldn't use her normal salon, just in case her stylist was ever questioned by the police. No, she would drive to a nearby city and have her hair cut shorter and coloured a darker shade with highlights. Examining her beautiful fingernails, she sighed. Yes, they would have to be short and plain. Less makeup. Sunglasses, and of course a floppy sun hat.

Timing was everything. She couldn't change her appearance too soon.

And an alibi. That was a critical detail.

She stood up and fetched her laptop, this time searching openly for a yoga and spa retreat to book under her legal, married name of Suzanne Hamilton-Forbes.

Once that was booked, she switched back to her incognito-mode browser and researched common poisons and poisonous garden plants.

The first choice that popped up was the ubiquitous garden shrub, the Oleander. With blooms of white, pink, peach, or red, it grew just about anywhere in Mexico. Every part of the plant was poisonous; the milky sap, the leaves, the seed pods, and the wood. Ingesting even a small amount could be fatal. The Oleander was a common cause of accidental death in coastal Florida where people used the wood to build a beach fire and roast hotdogs.

She tapped a finger on her bottom lip, a beach fire on the island was damn near impossible. Fires were actively discouraged due to the number of palapas, the grass-thatched structures common to many of the upscale homes owned by foreigners. If she used Oleander it would have to be ingested. It was a possibility, although an awkward option because she would have to put it into his food or beverages. If she got that close to her cheating spouse, she could just whack Brandon on the head and be done with it, witnesses be damned.

She clicked on the next option, Flores de Mayo, the Flowers of May, otherwise known as Plumeria, or Frangipangi. Beautiful, fragrant, and deadly. The milky latex sap was poisonous as well as being an irritant to skin.

No, still not effective enough, she mused, clicking onto the third choice.

Witches Weeds. Also known as the Moonflower, Angel's Trumpet, or Hell's Bells the plant contained alkaloids that cause deaths in humans and animals. A member of the Datura group of plants it has been used in various brews to commit suicide and murder.

Well, this was certainly interesting. She mused as she continued to peruse an internet article.

Some South American cultures have used Angel's Trumpet as a punishment for unruly children or to drug wives and slaves before they were buried alive with their dead lord. She snorted, *in this case the dumbass lord was the one who was going to be drinking the potion, not her.*

She grabbed a piece of paper and a pen, to copy the information provided by the website, including the basics on how to prepare the deadly brew. The internet was so helpful.

Unfortunately, all of these options required Brandon to ingest the poison, which meant she was going to have to attend the events at the music festival, and get close enough to him that she could spike his drink without him recognizing her. *A disguise. A really good disguise was essential.*

She scrubbed her browsing history, just in case her secret identity was ever discovered, and then closed the laptop. Feeling satisfied that she could pull this off, she decided to take a long leisurely swim in her indoor pool then perhaps a nap before a light meal and a glass of wine.

Life was good.

Chapter 2

January 31st Isla Mujeres

Mike Lyons pensively peered into the dark and cramped engine compartment then turned to Jessica Sanderson with a serious look on his face, "Just as I suspected, the chrome-reverse-sliding gear is broken," He said, with an emphatic nod.

"The what … is broken?" Jessica asked, one finely groomed eyebrow arched with scepticism. "I do know a bit about vehicles … and that … is pure bullshit."

Mike's eyes ignited with amusement. He held his hands palms-up and his shoulders scrunched upwards his earlobes. "That's the sum total of my golf cart knowledge." His spot-on imitation of a Gallic-shrug made him look like an apologetic Frenchman.

Jessica couldn't stifle her snort of laughter.

"Can I give you and Sparky a ride home?" Mike asked, a relaxed smile enveloping his face. A recent arrival on the island, Michael Lyons was, like Jessica, a Canadian. His Irish and Scottish ancestry had contributed to his thinning brown hair and green eyes flecked with bits of gold. A closely trimmed beard covered the bottom third of his face.

Jessica's pulse jack-hammered. He seemed trustworthy, but he was still an unknown entity.

Her previous and unplanned golf cart ride with a stranger had not gone well. In late May, she had survived a terrifying abduction and beating at the hands of Alfonso Fuentes, a Cancun drug lord who had become obsessed with her. With a gun shoved in her ribs, he had forced her to drive home where he attacked and battered her; injuring her ribs, face, and blackening both eyes. A combination of friends and local policía had saved her from further abuse or more likely a painful death.

She inhaled. Exhaled. And chewed her lip. "Okay, give me a minute to call my mechanic. I'll ask him to come rescue my carrito."

"You bet, take your time." Mike said, sauntering back to his rental cart.

Jessica punched the icon for Orlando's number and waited for him to answer. Through a mix of English and Spanglish she was able to describe where the cart was, and where she would hide the keys. "Thanks Orlando, I'm getting a ride home with Mike Lyons," she added clearly enough for her volunteer chauffer to hear.

Fifteen minutes later they stopped outside her home. Mike turned in the seat and asked, "Would you like to meet me for a drink tonight?"

About to decline the invitation she swallowed the lame excuse, saying instead, "Yes, thank you. That would be nice. Where?"

When she first met Mike, she had been sharing a quiet, healing moment with her pooch at the southern end of the island. She was sitting at the edge of the pathway leading down to the sunrise cliff at Punta Sur. The pain in her ribs and the facial bruising were healing, but the residual fear left her wary and hyperaware of her surroundings. A footstep on the stone stairway behind her caused Jessica to jump to her feet and spin around. Her heart pounded wildly. Her fists were bunched and ready to defend herself. She quickly assessed a possible escape route, running towards Garrafon park along the water-splashed, crumbling pathway. Not great, but it was an option.

As the man benignly studied her injured face she had blurted out, "You should've seen the other guy." She had hoped to sound tough and willing to defend herself if necessary.

He had appeared to be mildly amused at her caustic wisecrack and offered his hand when he introduced himself.

She ignored the polite gesture, until her traitorous dog Sparky had wagged his bristly tail and nosed the stranger's hand. Leaning in for a comfortable butt scratch, Sparky had aimed his blissful brown-eyed expression at her. *I think he's nice*, seemed to be his expert opinion.

Scowling at Sparky she had thawed, just a little, towards the man.

When she tentatively shook Mike's hand, Jessica had glimpsed the thickness of his wrist. He was solid, big-boned, and just naturally large, but not tall. He was probably not more than four or five inches taller than her five-foot-five frame.

Mike had glanced at her tight expression, and then at his hand and seemed to understand that she was uneasy. He quickly released his grip, and said, "I'll just get out of your way." He'd turned to climb back up the stairway. "Hasta luego," He'd said as he waved goodbye from the top of the cliff, letting her know that she was free to leave when she was ready.

Twisted Isla

Uncharacteristically timid, Jessica had been rooted in place for another fifteen minutes, until she heard several voices chattering happily in English. Listening to their conversation, she knew they were hoping to see the giant turtles mating in the confluence of the two currents at the end of the island. Feeling confident that nothing would happen as long as there were other people around Jessica scrambled up the dilapidated stairway. She popped up near the Maya ruin, startling the tourists with her sudden appearance. Waving hello to the group, she continued walking towards the entrance where her golf cart was parked.

Several times after that initial contact she had seen Michael Lyons, or Mike as he preferred to be called, at social gatherings on the island. He was pleasant, always smiling, and cheerful but kept his distance. Fine by her.

Today, when her cart had broken down halfway back from Centro, she had pushed the light vehicle off the tarmac and onto the dirt shoulder. She unlocked the seat and lifted it up. *Okay, now what?*

She checked the gas. *Lots.* She fiddled with and tweaked the various wires and belts. *Nothing.* Sparky was hot and panting, trying to hide in the small amount of shade beside the carrito. Then Mike had pulled his vehicle in behind hers and contributed his witty and useless appraisal of her problem.

Always ready for a ride Sparky had readily jumped into Mike's vehicle. With his long ears flapping in the cooling breeze, he was blissfully unaware that Jessica was primed, ready to scoop him up and leap out of the cart if she felt threatened.

Now, inside her bathroom Jessica mumbled through a mouthful of toothpaste. "Seriously Jess, get a grip."

She leaned over and finished brushing her teeth, then rinsed out the sink. She grimaced at herself in the mirror. When she was a teenager her dentist had talked her parents into braces for their only daughter. Several thousand dollars later her parents had said - enough. Sneaking up on thirty-years-old, her smile resembled every other North American female, straight, white, and even. Oddly, Fuentes' assault hadn't damaged her expensive dental work, making it easier to downplay the incident in FaceTime conversations with her parents in Canada.

With bright blue eyes, smooth skin and wavy blonde hair she strongly resembled her mom Anne Sanderson. She was slim, lightly tanned and reasonably fit. Her left arm, from shoulder to wrist, was decorated with a colourful design of tropical flowers, sea turtles, whale sharks and dolphins. Her long hair was braided in a single thick plait that either hung down her back, or more likely would drift over one shoulder and brush against her waist. On rare occasions, like when she had been the maid of honour for Carlos and Yasmin, she let it tumble in a curly mass.

Jessica blew a nervous breath. "You'll do," She said to her reflection. She had agreed to meet Mike, in an hour, for drinks at *Big Daddy's on the Beach*. She wasn't sure she was ready for this yet.

It's just a couple of drinks. You have to learn to trust again.

Chapter 3

January 31st Isla Mujeres

Yasmin Medina de Mendoza distractedly finger-combed her mass of dark corkscrew curls as she reviewed the invoices for the construction of their new pirate-themed restaurant. Expensive, was the word that came to mind. *No, really damned expensive was closer to the truth.*

Between their builder, the architect, Carlos, and herself, they had discussed and calculated the cost of the project endlessly, but until the invoices started rolling in, she really hadn't realized just how many concrete blocks, bags of cement, and concrete beams would be needed.

And this was just the basics. They hadn't even started working on equipping the kitchen or purchasing furniture or buying the endless necessities like cutlery, table lines, glassware, staff uniforms. Then there was the life-size pirate statue that Jessica insisted had to be stationed at the front door, to greet the customers. She said the figure needed to be about the size of the polar bears scattered through the island, advertising the ice bar.

Yasmin chuckled, the Ice Bar Isla was a ludicrous and surprisingly successful concept. Built completely of ice the interior temperature forced patrons to wear the cheesy winter parkas for photographs. Maybe Jessica was right, they needed a bit of silly fun to promote their new venture.

Picking up another invoice, she exhaled a short laugh when she read the name listed as the buyer; *A Pirate's Delight*. They hadn't actually settled on a name for the new restaurant because they kept coming back to this humorously inappropriate suggestion from Jessica. As Jessica had explained between gulps of laughter, the expression came from her not-so-correct grandfather. It was how he referred to a woman with a flat chest; a sunken treasure or a pirate's delight.

Yasmin had tried unsuccessfully to steer Carlos away from the name but like puppies with a new toy, Carlos and Diego just wouldn't let it go. Diego had immediately taken to calling their new venture the *No Boobs Restaurant*. Even the name *Treasure Chest* made them laugh, so she had been pushing for one of the other suggestions made by Jessica.

Men. Sometimes they had the maturity of a ten-year-old.

The new location was situated on the waterfront so *Hacienda Hideaway* wouldn't fit either, which left her with *Treasure Trove*. It was okay, but *A Pirate's Delight* would have been so much better had she not known about the double-entendre.

She leaned back, clasping her hands behind her head as she had seen Carlos do so often when he was puzzling over a difficult problem. Now she understood, that simple act reduced her neck pain. Her head had been tilted forward for hours, as she pored over costs and material delivery schedules. Her neck muscles were tight, her vertebra stiff. Being a business owner was no fun. She longed for her carefree days of being just an employee, oblivious to the hassles and stress that Carlos dealt with on an hourly basis as the owner of the popular *Loco Lobo Restaurant*. No, that wasn't true. She savoured her new life with Carlos Mendoza, stress and all.

Her eyes swept around the home that she shared with him, smiling at his man-cave decorating of black, red, and grey. After their wedding last February, she had intended to redecorate adding more colour and softness. But, with their decision to build a new waterfront restaurant and to try to have a family, fixing up their little nest was at the bottom of the to-do list.

Her cell phone woofed like a dog, signalling that Jessica was calling. "Hola seesta," Yasmin said, purposefully mangling the pronunciation. Jessica had been her best friend for several years and even though, since her marriage to Carlos, they didn't see as much of each other they were closer than most genetically-related sisters.

"Hola Yassy, what are you doing?"

"Playing at being a bookkeeper," Yasmin squinted at her laptop open to the spreadsheet where she had been entering invoice totals. The close work was giving her the mother of all headaches.

"That sounds really exciting," Jessica quipped. Her tone suggesting exactly the opposite.

"Si, it's very exciting," Yasmin said. She swiveled on the office-style chair, directing her gaze out of the window, "What are you up to?"

"Mike Lyons has asked me to meet him for a drink tonight," Jessica said, then fell silent.

"And ..." Yasmin prompted.

"And, I'm scared."

"Oh Jess, he seems like such a nice guy."

"I know. I keep telling myself the same thing, but my hands are shaking."

"When are you meeting him?" Yasmin's dark green eyes flicked back to the corner of her laptop, checking the time.

"In less than an hour. Forty-five minutes to be exact."

"Okay, Carlos and I are going to wander in and join you, unexpectedly of course."

"Oh my god, thank you Yassy, I truly am trying to get past this stupid fear."

"I totally understand, Jess. When Kirk Patterson attacked me a couple of years ago, it took me quite some time to deal with the fear and anxiety," Yasmin soothed Jessica. "What you went through was worse, much worse, but you'll get there."

"I hope so. I've never in my life been afraid like this."

"You have your entire island family supporting you." Yasmin replied. "We've got you, Jess."

"Gracias. See you soon. Love you."

"Love you too. Bye." Yasmin disconnected, then called Carlos.

"Hola mi amor," He answered.

"Hola my love. Can you leave the restaurant for a couple of hours?" She asked.

"Si. Problems?"

Yasmin quickly explained the phone call from Jessica, adding, "I said we'd spontaneously drop in for a drink."

"Spontaneously," He repeated with a laugh. "Mike is really going to believe that one."

"I know, but if he truly wants to get to know Jessica, he'll have to be patient. She needs time."

"Si, I agree," Carlos said, "I'll be home soon. I need to shower and change."

"Shower? Hmm. Maybe I need one too," She teased.

"In that case, I am leaving right now," He said.

She smiled when she heard the jingle of his keys as he picked them off his desk and gave them a deliberately hard shake close to the phone. "I'm waiting for you, big boy," She whispered. "Drive carefully."

"Wicked woman," He laughed and the sound warmed her.

Chapter 4

January 31st Isla Mujeres

Sitting at a table at *Big Daddy's on the Beach*, Mike Lyons slipped off his Ryder flip-flops and buried his toes in the still warm sand. His gaze was fixated on the narrow wooden walkway, squished between two small souvenir stores. The fingers of his right hand involuntarily tapped a tune that was running through his head. *Toes in the water, ass in the sand, not a worry in the world, a cold beer in my hand. Life is good today. Life is good today.* It was one of his favourite Zac Brown tunes that under normal circumstances would relax him.

She's going to cancel. I just know it. She'll text me any minute now, saying something's come up and she can't make it.

And then he saw her. Relief heated his veins as Jessica walked towards him. She was wearing a multicoloured, sleeveless dress that accentuated her fit body. Her delicate sandals were decorated with bright jewel shapes. Her glorious flaxen hair tumbled around her shoulders. Those eyes. As blue as the Caribbean Sea. He could feel his heart stutter. *She was stunning.*

Attempting to conceal his nervous delight Mike stood, smiled warmly and pulled out one of the chairs that faced the water view. "I can't do the gentlemanly thing and push your chair back into place," he said, popping one shoulder in a little shrug, "The sand prevents it from sliding forward."

"Thank you, Mike, I can manage," She said, flicking her eyes briefly to meet his. She dragged the chair a couple of inches closer to the table and settled herself. "This is my first time here. That sign post at the entranceway made me laugh," Jessica said, "You need booze and food. We need money. Let's help each other." Her lips lifted in a smile.

"It is funny," Mike agreed, then peered under the table. "I just noticed you didn't bring Sparky. Why not?" He shifted his eyes towards the waiter and signalled that they wanted drinks.

Jessica's reply was delayed by the arrival of the waiter. He asked, "What would you like to drink?

"A glass of Malbec, please," Jessica replied.

"Claro," He looked at Mike, "And you, amigo?"

"The same, por favor," Mike thought about ordering a bottle, but he didn't want to appear to be settling in for a long session of drinking. It would be less pressure on her to just to order by the glass.

Jessica waited until the server walked away before answering the question about Sparky, "I didn't bring him because I wasn't sure he'd be allowed. Some restaurants with outside seating areas permit dogs, others don't, plus the health department officials are starting to enforce the rules," She said. "I didn't want to cause a problem."

"Was he upset at you?"

"Of course. I got the sad-eyed, you-don't-love-me-look as I was getting ready," She imitated Sparky's doleful expression. "He'll make me pay for leaving him behind."

"How?"

"By demanding more golf cart rides."

As she talked about her dog, Mike noticed her posture and expressions were starting to soften. Maybe she would enjoy their evening after all. "Has your carrito been repaired?"

"Si, Orlando fixed the chrome-reverse-sliding-gear." Jessica said, light-heartedly, as she lobbed his previous one-liner back at him.

Mike tilted his head back and guffawed. "Busted. I know how to fix classic cars, but not an engine that looks and sounds like a lawnmower."

Jessica grinned at his remark, then changed the subject, "I like it here. Palm trees, sand, soft lights, and the country tunes."

"It has a nice relaxed vibe, although I imagine it will be crazy busy when the music festival kicks off in a few days. *Big Daddy's* is one of the main venues."

"Of course," Jessica said, giving her forehead a little tap, as if to say how could you forget that, "it starts on February 4th. I've lost track of time. For some reason I thought it started next week," She said. "It's a huge event now, but when it started in 2011 it was just three venues and I think four or five musicians. It also included a fishing tournament."

"Have you lived here that long?" Mike asked, surreptitiously studying her face. She was just so damn beautiful, yet she had no clue about the effect she had him.

"No, I've only been on Isla four years," Jessica said. "Many of my friends still talk about the good old days when the festival was first created by a group of foreign residents. They wanted to have fun and to help the community.

"So, tell me more about the festival," Mike said, hoping it would be a safe topic of conversation and nothing to do with kidnappings, drug lords, or murders.

"It started with a small group of people who wanted to fish, listen to country music, and contribute to the island. There were a couple of dozen big sport fishing boats that came down from various ports in the US for the event." Jessica paused and sipped her wine. "This is pretty good," She said, then continued, "Most of the money came from auctions of items like signed guitars, or a pair of Reba McEntire's jeans. Fun stuff. The fishing crowd were really generous with their bids."

Interested in the story, Mike propped his chin on his hand. "What do the funds get used for?" He had already bought tickets because he liked that type of music, but hadn't realized it was a fundraising event.

"Supporting the Little Yellow School House, the school for island children with disabilities."

"Huh, great idea."

"Are you attending any of the events?"

"Yep, I bought the full package. What about you?" He had actually paid for two complete packages, with hopes of enticing her to attend some of the events with him.

"I might try to squeeze in a couple, but everyone has to work at the *Loco Lobo* this week. We'll be slamming busy.

"Jessica!" A familiar voice called from the walkway, "It's great to see you here." Yasmin enthusiastically waved her long slender arm as she greeted her friend. Carlos stood beside her with a wry grin on his face.

Chaperones. Mike thought.

Chapter 5

January 31st Isla Mujeres

Mike liked both Yasmin and Carlos, so it wasn't a problem for them to join Jessica and he for drinks. He stood to greet them, kissing Yasmin on the cheek then shaking Carlos' hand. "Join us, please," He motioned to the two empty chairs.

Yasmin's eyes met his, "Thanks, Mike. We'd love to," She said, pretending their arrival hadn't been prearranged by the two women.

Carlos helped Yasmin with her chair, then he bent to buss Jessica's cheek, "How's my favourite trouble-maker?" He teased.

She exhaled a short laugh. "Whatever happened, it's not my fault. I didn't do it." She said, repeating her familiar bantering denial.

"What would you like to drink?" The waiter interjected, looking at the new arrivals.

Carlos looked at what the others were drinking and asked, "Is that a good Malbec?"

"Si."

"Bring two more glasses and another bottle por favor," Carlos said. He noticed that Yasmin and Jessica were occupied with discussing Jess's new dress. He quickly caught Mike's eye, and did a little side-roll in the direction of the women. *Yes, this was a contrived meet-up, but what could I do? Right?* His dark-brown eyes conveyed.

Mike grinned and slanted his head a scant inch. *Message received.*

"Did you hear about the armed robbery early this morning?" Carlos asked Mike.

"Yep, it's the hot topic on the island," Mike replied.

"I heard a gang attacked the Pemex station on Aeropuerto Road and smashed the safe right out of the wall," Jessica said, joining their conversation. She lifted her glass and took another sip of wine. "The news reports say it's the same gang that recently robbed gas stations in both Cancun and Playa del Carmen.

"Si, I read that too. Apparently three or four guys with balaclavas covering their faces used sledgehammers to remove the safe." Carlos leaned back in his chair, letting the waiter pour him a glass of Malbec. "It'll be fine, thank you," He said waving away the unspoken question of whether or not he wanted to taste the wine before accepting the bottle.

"That would have been really noisy. Why didn't someone report it?" Yasmin asked. "There at least three vacation homes near the Pemex station."

"They were all empty this week," Replied Carlos.

"Convenient," Mike stated.

"Good information more likely," Carlos said, then added, "They badly injured the nighttime employee."

"Oh no, did they shoot him?" Jessica asked.

"No, but the kid has a nasty concussion. One of the men cracked him a good one with the butt of his rifle. He has regained consciousness and was able to tell the policía what happened, but he will be in the hospital for a few days at least."

"Shit!" Jessica said, then peeked self-consciously at Mike. "Sorry, I've got potty mouth."

"You don't have to apologize to me for swearing. When I work on my old cars, I have a colourful list of profanities that I holler," Mike said. His broad smile pressed his cheek muscles upwards, scrunching his eyes into narrow slits. He resembled a round-faced Buddha.

"Don't you enjoy working on your cars?"

"Yep, I do. But they can be cranky old bitches when it comes to replacing parts. I've skinned my knuckles, mashed my fingers, and thumped my head too many times to count." He leaned forward, tilted his head and pointed at his thinning hair. "I don't have a lot of protection on top so I usually end up adding another scar to my collection."

"You do have an impressive assortment of dings and divots up there," Jessica agreed as she inspected his balding head.

"And, those are only the most recent ones," Mike added, straightening up again.

"I'm sure the gas station attendant will have a really nasty scar on his head," Yasmin said, bringing the conversation back to the robbery. "I hope he's going to be okay."

"I know his parents. I'll check with them tomorrow to see how he's doing," Carlos said, as he reached for the wine bottle. "Can I top anyone up?"

Jessica held her glass out, "I'll have a little more please." She grinned at Carlos, "I wonder if

Frick and Frack will be investigating the robbery," She said.

Mike Lyons looked puzzled, "Who's Frick and Frack?"

"My pet names for the two state policía detectives who always seem to be the unlucky ones assigned to sort out our Isla misadventures." Jessica answered with a wink at Yasmin, "Right, seesta?"

Yasmin didn't respond but the corners of her mouth inched up into a grin.

Mike quirked a dark eyebrow at her, "Misadventures, as in more than one?" He pretended he hadn't heard the island gossip about how Jessica and her mutt seemed to be involved in everything from illegal treasure hunting, to infuriating the local drug lords, to solving multiple murders. Much to Carlos' chagrin Yasmin was typically involved in the escapades.

"So, Mike, we don't know much about you, other than you mysteriously appeared on the island a few months ago," Jessica replied, completely ignoring his question. "Are you retired? Working? Hiding out from the authorities?

"Hiding out?" He sputtered.

"It's what tropical islands are famous for; people hiding from ex-spouses, the law, the tax collectors." She met his surprised look with the tiniest of smiles.

He belly-laughed, "Hell no! I am an independent winery consultant. I set my own work agenda by accepting or rejecting job offers."

Carlos leaned forward resting his forearms on the table, "Winery consultant. That sounds interesting."

"It is. I advise new owners how to set up an efficient winery, and how to make good wines." He said, "And I offer suggestions for existing wineries."

"Does it involve a lot of travel?" Asked Yasmin.

Mike smiled broadly, "Yes, it does. It's exactly what I love about the job. I've worked in Canada, the US, Australia, New Zealand, and I am considering a new contract offer in California."

"Where in California?" Jessica asked.

"I can't tell you specifically due to a confidentiality agreement."

Jessica smiled, "So, in the meantime you get to hang out on a tropical island and work on your tan."

"Yes, but I don't actually hang around on beaches," He replied with a grin, "I think my

Scottish-Irish ancestors had Roman centurion DNA in their genes. I was born with a light tan." He held out his forearm as evidence, displaying the slight olive hue of his skin covered with a mat of dark hair.

"Then why stay on Isla if you don't like beaches?" Jessica asked.

"I like the scenery," He replied, contemplating Jessica's magnificent eyes. *Yes, I like the scenery, a lot.*

Chapter 6

February 1st Cancun

"Woof!" A patrolman whispered as he strode past Detective Dante Toledo at the Cancun office of la Policía Estatal.

"Shut the hell up!" Toledo snarled at the retreating man.

"Ignore it, Dante, eventually the kids will get tired of ribbing us." His partner Detective Marco Cervera said, not bothering to look up or respond to the gibe.

"It's been eight damn months of listening to that stupid joke." Toledo complained. "Patrulla de la pata. Goddamn fricking *Paw Patrol*. All because of that mutt Sparky."

Cervera looked up from the stack of reports he was reading, "I don't like it either, but every time you react it fuels the fire. Just let it go." He sighed and ran his wide palm over his face, "it's no worse than our other nickname, los gemelos the twins." He said. He tugged at his tie, releasing its death grip on his thick neck.

When they first became partners, Cervera and Toledo had unintentionally settled on a preference for black suits, white shirts, and skinny black ties inspiring their nickname of the twins. Toledo resembled a younger Latino version of Tommy Lee Jones, Agent K in the spoof *Men in Black*.

Cervera dressed similar to his younger partner but stress and time had not been kind to his face. When he looked in the mirror, he saw a rumpled Basset Hound staring back at him; droopy brown eyes, sagging jowls, and earlobes that seemed to grow longer with each trip around the sun. He was coming up on his fiftieth birthday, but he thought he looked closer to sixty-five. *What did his dear wife, Beatriz, see in him?*

"Have you read this report about the armed robbery on our favourite island?" Toledo asked, holding up a piece of paper.

"No, as you have repeatedly pointed out to me, we are homicide detectives, not robbery, nor assault. Why would I read it?"

"Because it includes Isla Mujeres, and we know that sooner or later we will be interviewing the lovely Jessica Sanderson. She typically pokes her nose into every major incident on the island," Toledo replied.

Cervera picked up his cup of coffee. It was cold and the cream had formed an unappetizing scum on the surface. He set it aside, "I wonder why she attracts so many problems?"

"No clue, but she is a magnet for trouble."

Cervera nodded agreement then asked, "Is it my turn, or yours, to get the coffee?"

Toledo thought about that for a moment, "I don't remember, but I'll get it."

"Say hello to Amelia for me." Cervera said, his lips quirked up in a smirk.

"Amelia," Toledo uneasily glanced over his shoulder, "I have a better idea. I'll pay but you go get the coffees," He suggested holding out the cash.

"No, you need the exercise and your favourite barista, Amelia, is worried about your health," Cervera teased.

Muttering profanity, Toledo snagged his jacket from the back of his chair, shrugged it on, and stomped out of the policía bullpen.

Amelia, the teenage barista at their local café was infatuated with Toledo. She knew he was married but whenever he did the coffee run, she would greet him with a joyful smile and enquire about his health then lecture him on his eating habits. Typically, Dante would pretend to listen to her as he defiantly tapped three packets on the countertop, ripped off their corners and slowly poured the contents into his cup. Then he would thoroughly stir the coffee while nodding his head in agreement at her usual admonishment; sugar is bad for everyone.

Cervera grinned and dipped his eyes back to the stack of reports. The constant bickering between the partners was reminiscent of an old married couple, but Dante was right, the patrulla de la pata joke was getting stale and annoying. It had started with their last case involving Jessica Sanderson. Toledo was on his own one evening, and he had been invited for one of Beatriz' delicious meals. As they discussed the outcome of the case, Toledo mentioned that Jessica's mutt Sparky seemed to solve most of the crimes that had recently been committed on Isla Mujeres. He had joked about them working for Sparky, as part of the *Paw Patrol*.

Somehow the joke quickly spread to the other officers in the Cancun State Policía. Toledo vehemently denied that he had told anyone about his comment. The chilling possibility was their cell phones had been tapped.

Several months previously Marco's tech-savvy nephew had told him about the microphone arrays imbedded in electronic devices that gave various apps the ability to listen for keywords to refine what advertising was displayed on a person's laptop, smartphones, or electronic readers. He had questioned him thoroughly about the ability for others to listen-in to personal conversations. His nephew had verified that the microphones could be activated to do just that. It had alarmed Cervera.

As a detective de la policía it would be a big benefit to tap into criminal conversations, but he didn't want anyone listening to his phone calls, especially his boss. Neither Cervera or Toledo knew for certain where their Captain's loyalty lay – with the cartel, or against the cartel. Cervera's objective was to eventually retire from the State Policía, and not leave his lovely Beatriz a widow. Since the *Paw Patrol* incident, he and Toledo were extra cautious. When discussing sensitive information, they ensured their phones were off and tucked in a pocket while they quietly chatted face to face.

Curious about the robbery on Isla Mujeres, Cervera half-stood and reached across his desk, pinching his thumb and forefinger together he lifted the report from Toledo's pile. He sat back down and quickly scanned the information. When he read the amount that was claimed to be stolen, his head involuntarily snapped back in surprise. *Three hundred thousand pesos. Mierda! That was a lot of cash to have on hand.*

He leaned back in his battered chair and crossed one ankle over the other knee and let his mind run different scenarios. *Cartel?* That didn't feel right. In the leadership vacuum created by the death of Alfonso Fuentes, the *Los Zetas*, the old-school group that controlled Cancun, and the new kids on the block, *the Jalisco New Generation Cartel*, warred for control.

In the past there had been an unwritten code between the cartel boss and the police force; don't scare the tourists. Not because the gang-leader had any great sympathy for the vacationers, but because the violence would be splashed across the global news channels, especially the American television stations, warning tourists to stay away, and the cartel's best customers were the tourists.

The Jalisco New Generation Cartel had no such code. Their ruthlessness had caught the police and military by surprize, allowing them to seize control from the historic *Los Zetas*. However, as far as Cervera could see, robbing a gas station was too small-time for either cartel, even if the take was around sixteen thousand American dollars. Maybe the bosses needed more money to fund their war. Cervera huffed a terse laugh. *Not likely. They probably had rooms stuffed with money that needed laundering.*

Okay, who else? The Romanian gang that had been hacking the ATMs had gone quiet, for the time being.

Insurance claim? No, that didn't feel right either.

Insider job? That was more likely. Someone knew that money was going to be there although four armed men was overkill to subdue one unarmed teenager.

Cervera overheard Toledo's voice as he fended off raucous *Paw Patrol* wisecracks on his route back to the bullpen, so he smoothly replaced the report on his partner's desk then resumed scanning his own paperwork. He didn't want Toledo to gloat that he couldn't contain his curiosity and had read the statement. Beatriz often remarked that the two men behaved like adolescents. It was true, they did, but their teasing interactions helped relieve some of the stress of their job.

"And how was the lovely Amelia today?" Cervera asked, as Toledo set a fresh cup of coffee on his desk.

Toledo glowered at his partner. "She asked me if we had the perro named, *Chispita*, Sparky working with us. She had heard our unit had been renamed patrulla de la pata."

Chapter 7

February 1st Isla Mujeres

"Well, Sparkinator, what's on your agenda for the day?" Jessica asked, between sips of her second cup of coffee. Leaning one hip against her kitchen counter, she smiled down at her mutt. Sparky was short-legged and stocky with coarse terrier hair, Spaniel-type ears, and a dark racoon-mask around his eyes. His fur was a tweedy mix of black, white and grey with a brown bullseye on his rump, and a dark splotch on his left side. When he sat on his haunches, his front feet splayed outwards at a forty-five-degree angle.

Many people commented on how cute he was, and how fascinating his eyes were. He had, what her good friend Eileen Regn called, human eyes, with very visible white surrounding the dark irises. According to Eileen, nicknamed the Isla Fairy Dogmother, Sparky's eyes were an indication of some terrier in his genetics, plus he was smart, like a Jack Russell terrier.

Twisted Isla

The island pet gene-pool was a closed environment that mixed and remixed, time and again, and Jessica was pretty sure that Sparky had any number of breeds in his DNA. He could have anything from Labrador retriever, to poodle, to Chihuahua in his bloodline.

During his annual check-up a veterinarian had once marveled at the size of his package, commenting that even though he was neutered, Sparky was equipped like a Great Dane. Maybe so. She had seen a couple of long-legged canines on the island that definitely had a Great Dane ancestor so perhaps Sparky had some of that as well, but not the legs, definitely not the legs of that breed.

He also had an amazing sense of smell, so he could also be part beagle or bloodhound. His nose was frequently the cause of some of their more harrowing adventures, and he was the Sherlock Holmes that had unravelled a number of crimes. Frick and Frack, the two State Policía detectives had a love-hate relationship with her pooch, and if she was totally honest, with her as well. They resented her interference, but enjoyed the accolades from their superiors when a case was solved.

It didn't matter to her what Sparky's genetics were, but it would be fun to know a bit more about his history. She had thought about paying for a pet DNA test, but another friend had her island pup tested and the results came back as Mexi-mutt. Seriously? The testing company should have at least suggested other breeds, if only to make their customer feel as if she received value for her money.

And that reminded her of a discussion she had had with a tourist on Playa Norte early one Sunday morning. She was walking the shoreline with her pooch when a woman stopped her, then dropped to her knees in the sand to gently rub Sparky's ears.

Her eyes shining with pleasure, the woman had assured Jessica, "He's a beautiful example of a, PBGV."

"I'm sorry, a what?" Asked Jessica.

"A petite basset griffon vendéen. A French hound bred for their terrific sense of smell." The woman responded.

Feeling a bit naughty, Jessica had replied with a pithy, "No, he's not."

"Of course, he is," The woman retorted.

A half-grin tweaked the right side of Jessica's face, "No ... he's not."

The woman stood and dusted the sand from her knees with both hands before indignantly replying, "I," She emphasised, "have a petite basset griffon vendéen, and this dog," She pointed at Sparky, "is a superb example of the breed."

Trying really hard not to laugh, Jessica had responded, "He's a purebred Mexican low-rider."

"A what?"

Jessica had shrugged, and smiled, "He's a stray that I stumbled over in the woods."

"Well, I think you have a valuable, purebred that someone has lost," She scolded. "His owners are probably frantic. You should advertise on the internet that you have found him."

Jessica decided it was time to play nice. She smiled warmly at the woman, "Honestly," She said, "I've had him for a few years and he hasn't been reported missing. According to the local vet, he is just a handsome mix of many breeds."

The woman stared at Jessica for a long moment then made a noise of disagreement in her throat and trooped down the beach without saying goodbye.

Jessica looked at Sparky with a playful grin on her face. "I guess I could've gone along with her assessment that you are a valuable purebred, but I couldn't help myself. Her insistence that you are a petite-whatever made me stubborn."

Sparky's long pink tongue lolled over his teeth, he appeared to be grinning in agreement.

"Now, back to your plans for the day," Jessica said. She ran water into her empty coffee cup, and gave it a quick scrub before turning it upside down on the drain board. "I have to go to work in a few hours, so, first on the agenda is a carrito ride and swim for you, then a shower for me."

Recognizing the word 'carrito' Sparky grinned happily and his feet tapped out a salsa, while Jessica collected her keys, sunglasses, cell phone plus his harness and leash.

"Okay bud, let's go," Opening the front door Jessica lightly brushed her hand over the glossy turquoise paint. The colour never failed to make her smile. Scrunched in between two neighbouring houses in La Gloria, her modest casa was an eye-popping combination of orange exterior walls, vibrant pink window frames, and the blue door. Living on the Caribbean side of Mexico, she just naturally gravitated to vivid colour combinations. The interior was a bright and breezy mix of navy, turquoise, orange, yellow and pink.

Sparky impatiently towed Jessica towards *Frita Bandita*, the carrito that was their only mode of transportation. A couple of years ago when Yasmin had purchased a red Italika moto-scooter,

Jessica had been tempted to get one as well. And then she had found Sparky and she had decided that she wasn't coordinated enough to drive a moto with her dog balanced in the footwell like the locals. It was a common sight on the island. Sometimes the entire family piled onto the small motorcycles; two adults, two or sometimes three kids, and the family pet.

Jessica secured Sparky's leash around the steering column, to prevent him from toppling out of the cart on the corners. Next, she boosted her butt onto the grey vinyl seat and inserted the key in the ignition, then she turned a critical eye to the red and grey colour combination, "I think *Frita Bandita* needs a make-over," She said. "Perhaps something jazzy to match our house."

Sparky cast a quizzical glance at her. He seemed to be wondering why they were still stationary and not whizzing towards his favourite beach.

Jessica unhooked her sunglasses which were hanging from the vee of her top and settled them on her face. The sunglasses were a joke gift from her island-brother Diego Avalos. They could secretly record both sound and movement for whatever she looked at, saving the data onto a tiny memory chip that was embedded in the frame. She had tried it once, and thought the whole idea was hilarious, but a huge invasion of her friends' privacy and she had never used the recording feature again. The tiny on/off switch could be activated with just a light touch. She really should check the memory card just to see if she had accidentally recorded anything embarrassing.

Diego was such a joker.

Chapter 8

February 1st Isla Mujeres

Diego Avalos reached across the table and pretended he was going to tickle his youngest, Ana, who obligingly squealed with laughter.

"Nooo papi, don't tickle me," She screeched.

Wiggling his long fingers, "I'm … gonna get chu," His sneaky, slit-eyed look gave him a sinister air.

"No, no, no!" She shrieked, drumming her small feet against her chair.

"Diego, por favor, leave her alone," Cristina pleaded, cupping her hands over her ears, "Her screams are shredding my eardrums and I haven't had enough coffee to cope with this."

Muscular and broad-shouldered, with a twice-broken nose Diego resembled a Maya warrior until he smiled, and then he became a friendly giant. He grinned as he swooped four-year-old Ana off her chair and squished her in a tight embrace, peppering her face with butterfly kisses.

"Whose papi's beautiful girl?" He asked, beaming at his youngest daughter.

Ana coyly pointed at her mother, "Mami!"

"Really?" Tilting his head back Diego quizzically studied his daughter, then turned to his wife, "Did you bribe her to say that?" He asked.

Cristina winked and picked up the coffee carafe, pouring more into her empty cup, "It's secret girl stuff, you wouldn't understand."

Diego set Ana back on her chair, and kissed the top of her head. "Papi has to go to work, now sweetheart. You be good for mami, okay?"

"Si, papi, I'm always good," She turned her innocent brown eyes to her mother, "Aren't I always a good girl, mami?"

Cristina stifled a grin, "Yes, Ana, you are a very good girl," then she mumbled into her coffee cup, "most of the time."

Diego turned and pulled a light jacket from a hook on the wall, and tugged it on. The weather was forecast to be warm, sunny, and calm, but sometimes when he was out on the boat an ocean breeze would kick up and drop the temperature a few degrees.

Twisted Isla

Cristina's only brother, Pedro Velázquez, and he were partners in the *Bruja del Mar, the Sea Witch,* a fifty-eight-foot Viking sport-fishing boat. They specialized in photography dives all year-around, or in the summer months swimming with the whale sharks, but they would also take clients out who just wanted to fish. The yacht had cost more than the combined worth of both of their homes, but their high-end customers wanted luxury.

Every month it was a scramble, but so far, they were managing to make the payments, and take enough out of the business to support their families; in Diego's case Cristina and their four active youngsters José, Pedro junior, Luisa, and Ana.

And in Pedro's case he had just himself to support although he was generous with financial assistance for their aging parents. There could also be wedding bells in his future. Maricruz Zapata had captured his heart and he was hoping she would say yes, if he ever got up the nerve to propose to her. While he dithered Maricruz would probably pop the question first. She was a stunningly beautiful, no-nonsense lieutenant in the Mexican navy who was, for now, based on the island. That could change at anytime, she could be reassigned to any of the eight naval regions in Mexico, in the Caribbean, or the Gulf of Mexico, or on the Pacific

Ocean. If Pedro and Maricruz did move away it would leave a huge hole in their small and close-knit island family, but that was life.

"What type of charter are you doing today?" Cristina asked, drawing Diego's attention back to her.

"We have a repeat group from Germany who want to swim with and photograph the sailfish."

"Doesn't the music and fishing festival start soon?" She asked, tilting her head as if she was puzzled.

"Si, February 4th. Why?"

"With all those big boats out on the water using multiple-hook strip-dredges, and the deckhands tossing bloody bits of fish into the ocean to entice the predators to come closer, aren't your clients at risk? Won't the sailfish or the sharks confuse them with food?" Having grown up on the island and with her father, brother, and husband working on boats, she had a solid understanding of how fish behaved and how to catch them.

"Those events start in three days. We're okay for now," He replied.

"Okay, if you say so," Her raised eyebrows conveyed disagreement. "I think a few captains will be out there ahead of time chumming the water to bring the big boys closer."

"We'll be very careful. I don't want to risk losing this charter by suggesting it might be dangerous. It's a very lucrative one."

"Okay, just be careful."

"We will," Diego said, then placed both hands on her firm ass, and pulled her gently against his groin. He kissed her thoroughly, "Just so you don't forget me while I am working," He said, with a wicked smile then skimmed a guilty look at little Ana. She was occupied with her Cheerios and milk, fearlessly spooning the mixture into her mouth. The odd dribble escaped and landed on the table.

His heart lurched with love.

"Could you please leave?" Cristina prompted him with a little shove on his chest. "The pool-boy will be here soon and I don't want you to scare him," She dead-panned.

"Pool-boy? When did we get a pool?" He asked, surveying their three-room home that contained their bedroom, a bathroom, and a communal hammock-sleeping area for the four kids that also doubled as their living room and kitchen.

"It's out back, on our estate," She pointed at the fenced yard that was barely large enough for a table and six chairs, plus the small tree that cast a feeble shade over the play area.

"Ah. Yes. Our huge estate. I had forgotten," Diego replied. "By the way, Felipe and Alexis asked me a couple of days ago if we would be interested in dumping our kids for an adults' night out with them."

"That would be heaven. I'll call Alexis and find out when they are available, then I'll ask mom and dad if they will babysit for us."

"You could ask Pedro and Maricruz, just to see if they want the practice," He replied with a smirk.

"That would scare them into celibacy."

Chapter 9

February 1st Isla Mujeres

"I'm exhausted," Felipe Ramirez moaned as he turned the key, and then shouldered open the door on the modest casa that he shared with Alexis Gomez. Scraping across the un-painted concrete floor, the wooden door squealed as if it was in pain.

Her overnight bag clutched in one hand Alexis clamped her free hand over one ear, "Dios, Felipe, can't you fix that stupid door. It's dragging again."

"I know, I know. Last week's heavy rain warped it, again," Felipe sighed. "Just add it to our list."

"The never-ending list of things to fix," Alexis mumbled as she dumped the small overnight bag on their bed.

As per usual Felipe ignored her slight jab at his habit of letting the maintenance slide. They had been over this ground many times. He preferred to spend his free time relaxing rather than sweating over repairs. In Felipe's opinion this was a rental house and the landlord should be responsible for fixing stuff, not him.

"I'm getting too old for these all-night celebrations," He moaned, then dropped his overnight bag on the kitchen floor.

Her eyes tracked his movements. She bit down on the criticism riding on the tip of her tongue; a reminder that the bedroom was only ten steps away and the proper place to leave his bag.

"How many more quinceañeras do you have coming up in your family?" He asked.

"I think there are three more and then all of my nieces are done. They are exhausting, plus this time we had the three-hour drive back from Mérida." She conceded, but in truth she enjoyed the decidedly Latino custom of celebrating a young woman's fifteenth birthday and her entrance into womanhood.

Her own quinceañera had started at sunrise with pre-planned photographs that included her family and the priest. Next was an early morning mass, followed by a late-afternoon reception, an elaborate late-night dinner, then dancing and entertainment. By mid-morning of the following day the tired, overfed, and still-inebriated guests straggled home to their beds.

"Do you want a cervesa?" She asked. Her thick ponytail of straight dark hair swung in rhythm with her stride as she headed for the fridge.

"Si, gracias," He flopped into a nearby armchair. "Too bad we missed all of the action."

"Do you mean the armed robbery at the gas station?" She handed him a beer and slumped down in the other armchair. As always, the sight of the threadbare material irritated her, but their budget didn't allow for a replacement. Between the lack of sleep, the long drive from Mérida, and the general shabbiness of their dwelling, she was feeling cranky and petulant. She crossed her legs at the ankles and sipped her drink. It was best to keep her downbeat thoughts to herself otherwise she would just make Felipe irritable.

He raised the bottle to his lips and took a long, gulping swallow then wiped his mouth with the back of his hand, "Si, the only armed robbery in our careers and we weren't working. We missed all the fun."

"You have a strange idea of entertainment, Sergeant Ramirez." She quipped, referring to his title with the Policía Municipal de Isla Mujeres.

His large white teeth flashed in a grin. "Claro, Constable Gomez. I would have charged in with two big guns blazing, like Bruce Willis in *Die Hard*. I would have eliminated the bandidos."

Alexis rolled her eyes, "You only have one gun and I have a Taser. We are hardly in the same category as an imaginary American police detective."

Felipe flashed a cheesy smile at her, "But I'm better looking than Bruce Willis. Si?"

"Si, you are," She concurred, "But I am glad we weren't on shift or even on the island. We are, however, back on duty tomorrow morning at nine." She slowly pulled herself upright, and reached over to take his empty beer bottle from his right hand.

"Si, back to the grind. Twenty-four hours on, and twenty-four hours off," He sighed, and stood. "I need a nap. Care to join me?" He wrapped his well-developed arms around her compact body and nuzzled her neck.

"Nap?" Alexis leaned back against his arms and slanted her eyes to scrutinize his face, "Something tells me we wouldn't be doing much napping."

"It would help us relax, so that we could sleep," His eyebrows bounced suggestively. "Join me. Por favor," He mumbled as his lips found her mouth.

Leaning away from him, she pointed at the bathroom, "You stink of sweat and booze. Shower first, then I'll join you." She walked over to the front door and secured the latch. In this tight knit community, people habitually opened the door yelled a cheery greeting and walked straight in without waiting for an invitation to enter. There had been a few occasions when they had been caught in an awkward situation by overly sociable friends. It was better to be certain the door was locked.

She had known Felipe for six years, first as co-workers in the policía and now as lovers. Alexis knew he occasionally cheated on her with other women, but couldn't bring herself to end the relationship. If she split with him the situation at work would be difficult and she would be subtly pressured into quitting. The policía was a strongly male-dominated environment, where the female constables were accepted as long as they didn't stir up problems. Various forms of sexual harassment were to be tolerated, not reported. Infidelity was a man's birthright.

In the past three years she had gotten to know Jessica Sanderson a little better through the various incidents that she and her dog Sparky were involved in. Jessica had a very clear-cut view of how a man should behave in a relationship, and there were times Alexis could read the unspoken question in her eyes.

How can you tolerate his condescending chauvinism and his cheating?

The simple answer was if Alexis wanted to remain a cop she had to shut up and accept the situation.

She heard Felipe turn the shower on and she opened the bathroom door, "Got room for me?" She asked, unbuttoning her blouse.

Chapter 10

February 2nd Cancun

"How hard could it be for four pumped-up steroid-freaks to subdue one twenty-year-old?" The older man snarled, "One guy, and you almost killed him."

Bruno Torres remained silent, ignoring the slur about his muscular body. He wasn't a gym-rat, his regular job was in construction. Every fibre of well-defined muscle on his torso, arms, and legs had been acquired by hard physical work. He stood with his feet braced comfortably apart, his hands hung by his sides, relaxed and ready.

Tamping down his scorn at the fat lump sitting behind the desk Torres maintained a neutral expression. The stench of sweat in the tiny office was foul. Dark wet circles marred Rolando Chab's pale blue shirt. The man's nose was bloated and red, and his gut hung over his belt spilling onto his wobbly thighs. Eating and drinking appeared to be Chab's only physical activities.

Twisted Isla

"I hired you based on your success at similar jobs, with no deaths," Chab spat out the words.

"Verdad," Torres agreed, as he visualized their recent robbery on Isla Mujeres. He had pointed his assault rifle at the terrified employee and told him to shut up, then motioned to his crew to smash the safe out of the wall using their sledge hammers. He didn't waste his time demanding the gas-jockey open it. It was the type that employees could add excess cash to, but couldn't open. The kid wouldn't have had access.

Once the safe was free of the wall, Torres had smashed the butt of his rifle against the young man's head and the kid had silently toppled to the floor. Securing the victim's hands with plastic straps, he then fished in his pocket for a roll of duct tape, tore off a chunk then slapped it across the employee's mouth. He had checked the kid's carotid artery. His pulse was weak but he would probably survive.

As they were leaving one of his crew had angrily pointed out that he had dangerously misjudged the force of his strike and had seriously injured the young employee. The guy had crossly swiped the screen of his cell phone, calling in an anonymous report to the Red Cross, and asking for assistance for the gas-jockey.

"If that kid doesn't fully recover," He heard Chab's blustering, bringing his thoughts back to the present situation. "I'm holding you responsible," The man continued, aiming a thick finger at Torres' face.

Resisting the urge to grab the offending finger and bend it back at a sharp angle until it snapped like a twig, Torres calmly stared into Chab's rheumy eyes. In his peripheral vision he watched for any sudden movement of the fat man's hands. Rivulets of sweat trickled down Chab's face. The man swiped at it with his hand; a bear pawing away an annoying insect.

"What do you mean by that?" Torres quietly probed. His muscles tensed. The weight of his pistol itched against the small of his back. He was fast, but he didn't know if the other man had a pistol hidden under the belly fat that smothered his lap. His own pistol didn't have a suppressor but it was long after normal business hours and they were alone in the office. The trucking company was located on a remote road on the outskirts of Cancun where the noise of a gunshot wouldn't be noticed.

The older man's eyes widened, realizing that he had overstepped, "Nothing, I meant nothing," Chab sputtered. "I know the family and I'm concerned. That's all."

"Claro. Then I will collect our share and be on my way."

"Si, yes of course," Chab reached to open his desk drawer and felt the press of metal against his forehead. A vice-like grip pinned his hand to the desk. "I ... I ... need the key to my safe," He stuttered.

"Nice and slow, amigo. You don't want to startle me."

"No, no. I just need the key," His jowls vibrated with fear.

"Just push your chair back and move away from the desk. I'll get your key."

Chab suddenly panicked and thrust his hand deep into the desk drawer, scrabbling frantically.

Torres swiftly pulled his gun and squeezed the trigger, twice. One in the chest and the insurance shot in the forehead, "Estúpido pendejo," He sputtered as he wiped the gore off of his face and rolled the chair and body aside. He stepped away from the pooling blood, and fully opened the drawer. "Ah, a Beretta. And these must be the keys you were telling me about." He picked up two keys on a metal ring.

"Now, where would you hide a safe, amigo?" He sardonically asked the deceased.

"Well, look at this," Bruno Torres said, smiling at his good fortune.

After searching for an hour, he had been rewarded. Two safes. One for each key. The first one was about the size of a laptop and in an obvious location, behind a cheap painting in the dead guy's office. It was the decoy. It contained about ten thousand pesos in small bills. It wasn't a large amount of money and was probably the day to day operating float for the office manager.

The second one was in a storage room, tucked in behind an assortment of worn-out tools and junk. It was well-hidden, much larger, and oh, so much more fun to find. It had five neatly wrapped bricks of paper money, a few kilos of cocaine, and two more guns.

What the hell was Chab into? And if he had all of this stashed away why did he hire my crew to pull the Isla robbery?

Torres stared at the pile of loot for a moment, then made up his mind. This was his bonus. He found it, and he was going to keep it for himself. He had lived in the same dreary colonia in Cancun all his life and it might be time to do a little traveling around Mexico. He could dump his irritating girlfriend Gaby and her little brat, the one she insisted was his son. The homely little bastard didn't look a bit like him and he probably belonged to someone else that she was shagging on the side.

He counted out the share that he and his crew had been expecting to divide between them, putting it in a separate carryall. The rest of the booty he would stash under the spare tire in the trunk of his beat-up Tzuru sedan. He sorely missed driving his powerful Dodge crew-cab, but the robbery was too recent and he couldn't risk using it for a few months. The truck was hidden on Isla Mujeres at the hotel construction site where he and his crew worked six days a week.

Carefully wiping down any surfaces that he might have touched, Torres stepped out of the office, tugging the door closed.

Chapter 11

February 2nd Cancun

"Volunteers. Are we sure we have enough volunteers for all the venues?" Skip Bishop asked, as he scanned the Island Time Music Festival's organizing committee.

This collection of men and women both from the island, and from Nashville, were the organizational powerhouse that volunteered year after year to coordinate the annual music festival. From the beginning they diligently planned and managed, then during the festival they pitched-in and helped out wherever they were needed.

By the time the five-day event was over everyone of them was exhausted to the point of falling asleep on a bar stool, or dropping fully clothed onto their beds, mumbling, "I'm getting too old for this shit."

And yet when the first meeting for the next festival was called, there they were, eager and ready to do it all over again.

Skip ran his hand through his shock of hair without snagging any of his intricately carved rings on the long white strands. His untamed hairdo resembled Albert Einstein's distinctive mop with the addition of a little styling gel.

"*Big Daddy's* is looking for more servers, just to deliver drinks to the crowd," An attractive middle-aged blonde piped up. "We've put another ad on Facebook and our webpage to see if we can pull in a few more helpers."

"Great, thanks Julie," Skip replied. "Any other immediate challenges?"

"We had one homeowner who had to back out of providing complimentary accommodation for a performer. Her house sale completed sooner than expected," A broad-shoulder man said, "but we've found an alternate place."

"Thanks Rob," Skip said.

"The advance crew have arrived and are settled with their hosts. The performers start coming in tomorrow." Another voice offered.

"Awesome. Just two more sleeps 'til show time!" Skip hooted with delight.

Chapter 12

February 2nd Isla Mujeres

Mike Lyons tapped his left palm with the two VIP all-inclusive packages that he had purchased for the events kicking-off in a couple of days. He had spent a lot of money on the passes, but even if he didn't get full value out of the tickets the money would go to a good cause. He was more concerned that Jessica would think he was pressuring her.

"Ah screw it!" He said, then picked up his keys and headed out the door. "Nothing ventured, nothing gained."

Hunting for a parking spot he navigated his rental golf cart through the afternoon crush of day-trippers visiting the island from the hotel-zone in Cancun. Fifteen minutes later he wheeled in behind the Casa de Cultura on the malecón, and stopped the little vehicle. He hopped out, and secured the anti-theft cable.

Golf carts weren't normally stolen especially during the day, but most of them were the same plain vanilla colour and there were only six different keys for all of the models. Many were taken by accident. It had happened to him once at the parking lot by the Ultramar passenger ferry. When he decided that he would extend his stay on the island, due to a chance meeting of a certain blue-eyed blonde, he had gone shopping in Cancun, stocking up on more t-shirts and shorts. On his return he discovered his cart was missing but a similar one was parked near where his had been.

Flummoxed, he walked across the parking lot chat to the attendant. Just as he started to explain his dilemma an embarrassed local returned with his vehicle, repeatedly apologizing.

"Lo siento. Perdón, I thought this was mine," He patted the passenger seat. "Hop in. I'll drive this one back to my cart then she's all yours."

Offering his hand to Mike, the man had introduced himself as José Martínez, a name about as common in Mexico as Joe Smith was in Canada. They had laughed at the mix-up, switched vehicles, and parted on friendly terms. Now, whenever José spotted Mike, he hollered a greeting.

Mike pulled on the security cable to ensure it was latched, then pocketed the keys and headed in the direction of Hidalgo Avenue. Jessica should be starting her afternoon shift at the *Loco Lobo*

Restaurant. He noisily sucked up air, and slowly exhaled. *Relax idiot. Don't act like an anxious stalker.*

"Incoming," Yasmin said, winking at Jessica. She motioned with her chin towards the main entrance.

"What?" Jessica asked, turning to see what Yassy was talking about.

"Hi, Jess. Hola Yasmin." Mike said, lifting his hand in greeting.

"Hi Mike. Good to see you," Jessica felt a tickle of pleasure skitter up her spine. "Are you hungry or thirsty?" She asked, pointing to a table with a menu.

"Both," He said. Jessica watched him fiddle with a chair adjusting the position a couple of times, before he decided to sit. "I'll have a Sol first while I check the menu."

"Coming right up."

She returned with his beer, and set it on the table. "Do you need more time to decide?"

"No, I'm good, Just a *Loco* burger please." Mike said, closing the menu and handing it back to Jessica.

"Single or double?"

"Better make it a double."

"Fries with that?"

"Only if you have the sweet potato fries, those are my favourites."

"Yep, we do. They're my favourites too." Jessica smiled then walked away. He was edgy. His right knee jiggled a few times before he put a hand on it as if to stop the unintentional movement. As Jessica punched Mike's order into the terminal, she could feel his eyes following her movements.

Mike sipped his beer and chatted briefly with the patrons at the table nearest him, mostly about the weather and the upcoming music festival.

Jessica noticed he frequently glanced in her direction. *Something was definitely on his mind.*

Twenty minutes later Jessica returned to his table with his order, "Do you want another beer with your meal, Mike?"

"Sure, that would be great." He handed her his empty bottle, then picked up one half of the huge hamburger and bit into it. Sauce gushed out and oozed over both of his hands. "Well, damn," He muttered. His cheeks turned a rosy pink as he put the slippery jumble of two meat patties, cheese, tomatoe, lettuce, and bun back on his plate.

"Sorry about that, it happens to everyone," Jessica said, handing him a stack of thin paper napkins. "I keep telling Carlos we need to cut back on the condiments, but he says everyone expects his hamburgers to be flavourful and gooey."

"At least it didn't get on my clothes – yet," He said, sheepishly scrubbing the flimsy napkins between his fingers.

"Do you need more napkins?" She asked preparing to reach for another stack on a nearby table. "They're annoyingly tiny, and they quickly disintegrate."

"No thanks, I think I got the worst of it." He heaped the soggy, shredded paper at the edge of his plate then looked up at her. "Have you got a minute, Jess?"

"Sure," She leaned one hip against the table and smiling at him. *What the heck is he so worried about?*

"I have a small problem that I was hoping you could help me out with."

"Happy to help, if I can."

"A buddy of mine has a family emergency and he had to return to Canada. He gave me his all-access package for the music festival and asked me to find someone who could use it."

"Wow, that's too bad. Those packages are expensive. I can ask around and see if someone wants to buy it."

"Well, actually, I was wondering if you would like to have it?"

"Me?" Jessica eyebrows popped up towards her hairline, "I'm really sorry, Mike. As much as I would love to, I don't have that kind of money to spend on entertainment."

"My buddy doesn't want any money; he just wants someone to enjoy the festival," Mike quickly explained. He reached into one of the deep, side-pockets of his Hook and Tackle shorts and pulled out the bundle of passes and wristbands. "Would you like to have them?"

Studying his earnest expression Jessica bit her bottom lip to suppress a laugh. *My buddy. My ass. Mike was asking her out, and was afraid that she would say no.* "Thanks Mike, that would be great," She said, taking the offered gift. "Please tell your friend thank you so much, but I can't go to all of them. We'll be super busy and I'm scheduled to work the afternoon shift all week.

"That's okay, he'll be happy that the passes aren't going to be wasted," He said, then added, "Maybe we'll run into each other at some of the venues."

"I'm sure we will," Jessica said. "Can I bring you something else instead of the hamburger?" She asked tilting her head at the oozing heap on his plate.

"Er, no, that's okay. I have an appointment, so maybe you can just package this up to go and bring me the check."

"Absolutely," Jessica said, scooping up his plate.

Ten minutes later she returned with the to-go parcel, and the bill. "Here you go."

"Thanks Jessica," Mike said, quickly glancing at the amount and tossing down enough to cover a generous tip. "I'll catch you later, at the festival."

"Sounds good," Jessica agreed. As she watched his retreating back, she sighed, "Mike, Mike, Mike. What am I going to do about you?"

A few paces along Hidalgo Avenue, Mike spotted a garbage can and tossed his take-out order into it, "Smooth move, dipshit. Real smooth move." He grumbled.

Chapter 13

February 3rd Cancun

Toledo shifted his feet, easing a cramp in his leg, "How many corpses have we stood over, waiting for the coroner to confirm death?" He asked Cervera.

"Too many to count," Cervera grunted. "There's no doubt about this one, he's dead," He said surveying the gore.

"No, no doubt at all. Two shots; one in the chest and one a direct shot to the head at close range." Belatedly, Toledo turned his head and looked over his shoulder to confirm that the office manager, Valeria Flores, wasn't within hearing range.

"What do we know about him so far?" Asked Cervera.

"According to señora Flores, his name was Rolando Chab López and he was the sole owner of Halcón Logistics. The company is licenced to transport goods throughout Mexico and the USA," Toledo took a quick peek at his notes. "She stated that she arrived at her customary time of eight in the morning to open the office. She was the one that discovered her boss, and placed the 911 call."

When she had calmed down sufficiently to ask her questions, she babbled through her tears that she had noticed that her boss's car was parked in his reserved slot beside the front door. According to señora Flores, he typically didn't arrive until an hour later. She had made coffee, preparing him a fresh cup and tapped on his door before pushing it open. Seeing the headless body, she screamed and dropped the coffee, splattering her legs and feet. The horror of what she was looking at obliterated the pain of the hot liquid.

Cervera had no doubt she would be reliving this nightmare for many months if not years. He hoped she would seek professional help, or she might never get over the trauma. The police department certainly couldn't or wouldn't provide assistance to her.

Noticing a commotion at the loading dock he held up one finger, "Wait here for the coroner. We have a problem. I see a group of drivers arguing with señora Flores."

"I'll call the sergeant and confirm the uniforms have patrol cars blocking the gates," Toledo said.

"Bueno," Listening to Toledo radio the sergeant, Cervera headed straight towards the knot of men surrounding the woman. "¿Que pasa?" What's happening?"

"The men want to start work, señor Cervera," She said, "but I told them they should speak with you before leaving."

"Verdad," He agreed, addressing the grumbling drivers, "I must speak with each of you before you leave."

"We don't get paid for standing around," A large man protested loudly.

"I'm sure you want to help solve the murder of your boss, right?" Cervera asked.

"I don't care about that cheap pendejo," Another man griped.

Cervera shot Valeria Flores a quick questioning glance. *What's that about?* She avoided his eyes, staring at the tarmac. *Interesting.*

"Lo siento. You'll have to be interviewed before you leave. I'll radio headquarters for additional help to speed up the process." Cervera put his fists on his hips, exposing his service pistol, "Now, park your rigs, and shut them down. No one is leaving until I say so."

As the men slowly moved away, he heard several crude comments about his mother and his ancestors. He'd leave those drivers to the last and give them his special attention. Turning to retrace his steps to the murder scene Cervera noticed the coroner's vehicle squeezing through the partially opened gates. He was glad to note the constable quickly closed and secured the gate as soon as the back bumper was clear.

Cervera waited until the doctora had stopped her Nissan Altima, then reached out and opened the car door for her. "At your service, Doctora," He mock-bowed and reached for her hand, as she lifted her eye-catching leg out of the car, and set her foot on the ground. He noticed that she was wearing her customary figure-hugging dress and her high-heels. She was beautifully attired, as an affluent Méxicana must always be.

"Muchas gracias señor," Doctora Fabiola Maldonado replied. Meeting his eyes with a playful grin, she stood up and asked, "What special gift do you have for me this time, Marco?"

"Gunshots, one to the chest and one to the head. Quite possibly the gun was pressed against his head when fired," He answered in cop-speak.

"Suicide?" She closed the car door, and unnecessarily beeped the locks. The trucking compound was secure, but it was her routine.

"Two gunshots? Definitely not suicide, unless the victim had an abnormally high tolerance for pain."

"Ah, then since you have it all wrapped up, there is no need for my expertise," She turned and put her hand on the door handle of the Nissan, as if she was preparing to leave.

"My dear Fabiola, I am always delighted to see your exquisite visage, and to be educated by your eloquent words." He crossed his palms dramatically over his heart, "I beg you please stay and enlighten your ignorant servant."

Chuckling the doctora said, "Marco, you can be such a pendejo. Let's see if you guessed correctly."

"Guessed? Now, I am insulted," He demurred. "This way," He pointed at the office door.

Carefully stepping inside the foul-smelling office, Fabiola warmly greeted Toledo, then tugging on her nitrile gloves she focused her concentration on the corpse, "Yes, dead. That's one point to you Marco."

Toledo flicked an amused expression at Cervera.

"And upon closer examination I'm willing to concede the second point to you as well. Not suicide. Murder." She straightened up, and tilted her head at Cervera. "Well done, perhaps you would like to join my team as an apprentice."

"Gracias for your kind offer, but no thank you!"

"We'll transport him to the morgue and let you process the scene. Is there anything in particular you want me to look for?"

Cervera's face twisted in thought, then he shrugged, "How about the killer's name, physical description, phone number, and home address for a start?"

Doctora Maldonado sighed, and turned to Toledo, "How do you put up with him?"

"It's simple. If I'm unkind to Marco, my wife and I don't get invited to dinner," Toledo said, "And I love Beatriz's cooking." He looked at his partner and waggled his hand back and forth, "Him, not so much. But I have to take the bad with the good."

The coroner grinned at Toledo's cheeky assessment of the situation, then turned back to her gruesome task.

Chapter 14

February 3rd Cancun

Two hours later, and three cups of a foul-tasting liquid that was rumoured to be coffee, the detectives had only learned that the dead man was not well-liked. He was rude, arrogant, cheap with wages, and free with his hands around the female staff. No one, other than Valeria Flores, was upset about his death, but then she had discovered the grisly mess. The drivers and warehousemen were more concerned about when they would be paid for their hours worked, and who, if anyone, would take over the trucking operation. As each employee had been interviewed and their personal contact details verified, they had been allowed to leave the compound.

Toledo rolled his neck, listening to the creaks and pops of his vertebra. "I need take a leak, and to walk around for a few minutes."

Cervera merely grunted that he had heard. His concentration was on a sheet of paper littered with names, and circles, and stars; the musings of his analytical mind.

Toledo pushed open the door on the men's bathroom. It was the expected filthy disorder of a communal toilet used by many men, and only cleaned by the female staff when they couldn't stand the stench any longer. He pissed, zipped up, and moved to wash in the sink. The filth extended to the sink bowl, and the taps. *No, not touching that.*

He sighed, and ambled into the warehouse area, passing a pile of impact wrenches, tire irons, and drills. He stopped, retraced his steps and frowned. Something tickled at his brain. "Hey Marco," He shouted.

"Si, ¿que pasa?"

Toledo pointed at the stack of tools, "Does that seem like a good way to store expensive tools? Wouldn't the mechanics want them more accessible?"

"I don't know. This place isn't exactly clean."

"Forget the bathroom, the rest of the place really isn't that badly organized. Check the mechanics' workbenches."

Cervera eyed the workbenches. "Claro, okay, so they look organized."

"Then why are these piled here?" Toledo said, carefully stepping through the jumble, then stopped, "Interesting."

"What?"

"A safe, a much larger safe than the open one we found in the office."

"Is it open?"

"Yes," Toledo leaned forward and shone the flashlight from his cell phone into the dark cavity, "And ..." He paused to reach inside and swipe a finger through a fine white powder, then he held it up for his partner to see, "it's empty, except for this."

"Drugs," Cervera exhaled a long and tired sigh.

"Si, cocaine," Toledo confirmed by touching the end of his finger to the tip of his tongue.

"Señora Flores has some explaining to do," Cervera motioned with his head in the direction of the office. "Let's have another chat with her."

Toledo and Cervera resolutely marched back to her tiny work space in the reception area.

Valeria Flores blanched. She felt sick. *Madre de Dios.* They looked fierce. Gone was the affable basset hound demeanor of the older one, Detective Cervera. He now resembled an alert Rottweiler, his dark eyes raking over her face.

"Is there something else you wanted to tell us, señora Flores?" He stood behind the chair that sat in front of her desk, gripping the back with both of his wide hands. The plain wooden seat was provided as a courtesy for visitors but, in his mitts, it had the appearance of a weapon, as if he might pick it up and strike her.

She sank onto her chair and propped her elbows on her desk, her head resting in her palms. "Si, lo siento," Her voice trembled, "I didn't tell you everything." She aimed her words at the desk, afraid to meet the glare of the detective.

"Perhaps you would like to explain your little omission now?" Cervera said, glaring at the top of her head.

"What was in that second safe?" Toledo demanded.

"Money, cocaine, and two pistols," She mumbled.

"What was he involved in?" Cervera asked. He was deliberately trying to ramp up the tension, snapping out questions; first Toledo, then him, then Toledo again.

"His trucking business was losing money, a lot of money," She said, reaching for a tissue, and dabbing at her eyes. "Someone from the cartel approached him and he agreed to transport drugs." She loudly blew her nose, and dropped the soggy tissue in the garbage can beside her desk.

"Across the border?"

"Sometimes, but primarily inside Mexico."

"How long has this been going on?" Toledo bounced the next question at her.

"Only a few months."

"Was the relationship working out?" Asked Cervera.

"I thought it was, but now this happened," She replied, unable to say the words to describe the horror that she had seen. He hadn't been the kindest boss, but no one deserved to die like that.

"We don't have any proof, yet, that the cartel was responsible for his murder," Toledo stated.

"Valeria lifted her head, a puzzled expression on her face. "But who else would do such a terrible thing?"

Cervera blew out a tired sigh, "Unfortunately, señora, many people will kill for drugs, or money, or guns." He replied, "Even family members or one of his employees."

"You can't seriously think one of us would do this?" She stammered.

Toledo silently pinged a look at Cervera, *you can answer that one.*

Cervera pinned her with his glare, "We always investigate those that are closest to the victim, first, and work from there." He reached into a pocket and pulled out his card, "Here is my contact information. If you think of anything, and I do mean anything, that you have neglected to tell us, call me. Immediately."

"Am I under suspicion?"

"As I said, we start with the closest and work outwards," Cervera's lips tweaked in a tight smirk. "Please, do not leave Cancun."

"But the drivers, you let them leave. Some have routes that take them across Mexico or into the USA," She said. "If one of them killed Rolando, they could just abandon the truck and disappear."

"That was before we knew about the second safe, and the missing money and drugs," Cervera reminded her. "So, you see señora Flores, we are a little annoyed that you have already hampered our investigation, and perhaps your deception has allowed the murderer to escape."

"I'm very sorry," She whimpered, "I was terrified."

Cervera pulled open the passenger's door of their unmarked sedan and pushed his bulk into the car. They had left the windows rolled down but the interior was still stifling hot, and it was only early February. One of these days, he was going to demand a car with air conditioning. One lucky day, before he retired.

Toledo turned the key in the ignition and the car reluctantly grumbled awake. He turned to Cervera, "Did you catch the comment when she referred to the jefe as Rolando."

"Si, at first it was señor Ramírez, and then suddenly she refers to him by his first name."

"You think they had something going on?"

"Maybe, but I don't think she had anything to do with his murder."

Chapter 15

February 4th Isla Mujeres

"Hola! Brandon, over here," Yelled a friendly female voice.

Brandon Forbes turned in the direction of the shouted greeting, smiling at the sight of an older woman waving vigorously at him. She was standing beside a large wooden sign set into an anchor, proclaiming that he had arrived on Isla Mujeres.

"Brandon, over here," She repeated.

"Hey y'all, are you my ride?" He asked, sauntering towards her.

"You bet, honey. I'm Michelle. My golf cart is in the parking lot," She said pointing to her right.

"Pleased to meet you Michelle. I guess y'all know my name is Brandon Forbes," He briefly shook her hand. He chuckled when he spotted her vehicle. It was decorated with tinsel and assorted gewgaws and a welcome to the Island Time Music Fest banner was attached to the side.

"You just hop right in here and I'll take you to your assigned accommodations." She smiled, and patted the front seat of the vehicle.

Brandon reached back and placed his carryon on the rear seat. He hoisted his butt onto the front seat and stood the guitar case at his feet. "Thanks for the lift."

"My pleasure, sugar, it's what we do. We try to make your life easier during the music festival," She smiled, then nodded at the guitar, "Is this all you have?"

"Yes ma'am, this is it. I usually travel light," He flashed his signature dimpled grin, the one that he knew drove the women wild. "A couple of fellas met our group at the airport with a van. The bigger pieces of equipment will be delivered to the venues, and now here I am, being offered a ride from a very pretty lady." She was at least as old as his mom, or maybe as old as his great-auntie Jean, but every woman appreciates a man who smiled at her and said nice things.

"Well aren't you just a sweet thing," Michelle responded with a laugh and a wink that clearly communicated that even though she enjoyed the compliment she wasn't fooled by his flirting, not

Twisted Isla

one bit. She turned the ignition key, put her foot on the gas pedal. "Is this your first time on the island?" She asked.

"No ma'am, I was part of the festival last year too. To be honest I didn't see much of the island. I was too busy," He said without explaining exactly what he had been busy doing. He'd spent the entire week singing and screwing with the occasional break for food, and of course, copious amounts of alcohol. He was planning on a repeat performance this year.

"The house where you're staying is on the western side of the island, right on the beach. You'll love it!" She said, as she passed the parking lot attendant a few pesos. The barrier lifted, and Michelle merged into the steady stream of vehicles.

"Is the house a long way away?" Brandon asked. He had been hoping to be right in the thick of things where there would be a steady supply of females.

"Just a couple of miles from *centro*, but a golf cart has been dropped off for you to use."

"Awesome," He swung his head around taking in his surroundings, "but, there surely seems to be a whole lot of traffic."

"You'll get used to it."

Twisted Isla

In an attempt to make conversation and because he was mildly curious Brandon asked, "Why is the island so busy?"

"Northern folks escaping the cold winters. And Carnaval usually happens in February or March. Plus, the music festival has become a huge attraction," She said. "I love the energy and the vibe."

Watching the stream of golf carts, scooters, cars and even bicycles flowing around them, he asked, "Doesn't it scare you driving in this chaos? No one stays in their lane. They're all dodging and weaving."

Michelle shot him a brief look, "No, it's fun. As my one of my Canadian friends says, driving in Mexico is like playing a video game. It's an adrenaline rush and you need quick reflexes."

"I can see that," Brandon steadied himself by grabbing the metal roof support, as she dodged around a moto-scooter. "Three people … on a scooter?"

"Honey, that's nothing," Michelle laughed, "I've seen two adults, three kids and a mutt. Or two guys, with one dragging a wheel-barrow behind. Or two guys carrying a really long extension ladder. Or my favourite, the wife clutching a four-foot round table, and hanging on by tightly squeezing her thighs against the seat."

"Seriously?"

"Seriously. Motos are used like trucks. If you can balance and drive, even one-handed, you're good to go."

The vehicle suddenly jolted upwards then slammed back to the pavement. Brandon yelped, "Shit! Did you just run over an animal?" He turned and searched the roadway behind them. *Nothing.*

"Sorry hon, I forgot to warn you about the topes."

"The what?"

"Speed bumps. They're all over the island." She lifted a hand and pointed ahead, "See, look ahead, we've got lots more to cross. I'll slow down a bit."

"No problem. I just wasn't expecting to be bounced off the seat," He said. "I just noticed that you don't have a wind-shield or windows. What do you do when it rains?"

"Get wet," She tossed him a quick grin. "Golf carts hate the rain, so the best solution is don't drive in the rain. A sprinkle, that's okay. But a tropical rainstorm. Uh-uh. Not good."

"What happens?"

"When it rains, it really rains. The streets flood, the drains can't take the water away quickly enough. The motor stalls and there you are stranded in the middle of the road," She laughed. "It's a pretty common sight to see soaking-wet people pushing a cart out of a deep puddle and over to the curb."

"What do you do if you get caught in a rainstorm?"

"Pull into the closest bar and order a frozen margarita."

"I like your style, Michelle," He said leaning over and lightly touching her arm. "Are you sure you don't want to be my personal chauffeur?" He teased.

Chapter 16

February 4th Isla Mujeres

The heat of the late-afternoon sun warmed her shoulders as Suzanne Hamilton-Forbes stepped off the yacht onto the private dock. Her flight into the Cancun International Airport had been smooth and fast in her eight-passenger Phenom 300E jet. In the past some of her fellow pilots had said that she was crazy to fly single-pilot, but she enjoyed the freedom. Flying solo had the added benefit of privacy.

After clearing customs with her fake passport, in the name of Sophia Hayden-Smith, of Dallas Texas, Suzanne had met the driver of an exclusive limousine service outside the terminal entrance. He had whisked her through the chaotic, no-holds barred Cancun traffic from the airport to a secluded marina. At the marina the captain had welcomed her aboard his yacht and transported her across the bay to the southern end of Isla Mujeres, the Island of Women.

Twisted Isla

It had been a relatively stress-free journey and she was pleased that she had arrived at her final destination before sunset. Tropical sunsets were usually a brief and vibrant spectacle of brilliant oranges, reds, and purples. She was looking forward to savouring a large glass of wine while watching the display. Then she would enjoy more wine and a meal, pre-arranged when she had made the booking, although her expectation of fine cuisine was probably foolish. At least the wine would be pleasant, if, and it was a big if, they had purchased the wine that she had specified.

Disembarking at the wharf the deckhand offered his hand and she ignored the gesture. He was probably hoping for a tip, but as far as she was concerned the rental agency could deal with that. Without speaking she strutted up the dock, confident that *someone* could manage to bring her two Gucci valises up to the house.

The path from the wharf to the house was an annoyingly long climb of several levels of concrete stairs making her decision to wear her comfortable Louboutin loafers a good choice. She couldn't imagine trying to hike up these stairs in heels. Surely some of their clientele were older and not able to navigate the steep incline. Why hadn't the owners installed an elevator? *Ridiculous!* No matter, she would only be here a few days just long enough to deal with her errant spouse.

I wonder what my darling Brandon is screwing this time? Redhead? Blonde? A brunette? Definitely someone with large breasts. He was definitely a boob man, there was no doubt about that. He was due to perform soon, but she wasn't ready to deal with him - yet.

"Bienvenida señora Hayden-Smith," said a diminutive dark-haired woman. "Mi nombre es Luz Hernández. Soy tu asistente."

The new client strode past her, "Speak English, or I will contact the agency and get another maid."

"Certainly, my name is Luz Hernández," Luz replied, dropping her chin towards the floor to hide her expression. "How may I assist you, madam?"

"Have someone bring up my suitcases. Where is the master suite?" the woman snapped.

"It's just inside on your right," Luz said. She walked towards the house and pointed at the spacious suite.

"What, not on the top floor?"

"If madam would like, you may use any of the five bedrooms, but the one on the main floor is the largest with the best view. It also has a glass wall that opens out to the swimming pool," Luz replied.

Suzanne marched inside to the bedroom. "It's small," She sneered, "but it will have to do."

Behind her Luz's eyebrows rose up in surprise. *Small? The master suite was larger than the house that she shared with her esposo and three sons.*

Out on the water a horn tooted a couple of friendly blips. Luz shaded her eyes against the brightness of the sinking sun and scanned the bay. A large white sport-fishing boat, that looked like Diego and Pedro's *Bruja del Mar*, was cruising past. Someone was standing on the aft-deck waving at the captain of the private launch that had brought *la señora* to the house.

Luz could see Hau lift an arm in acknowledgement as he powered past the stern of the other vessel. Pulling a deep breath though her nose she considered her newest client, Sophia Hayden-Smith.

This was going to be an interesting two weeks with la señora.

Twisted Isla

On the *Bruja del Mar*, Diego turned and climbed the ladder to the upper steering station.

Comfortably braced in front of the captain's chair, Pedro lightly rested his fingers on the wheel. One arm was propped near the controls. "Was that Damien Hau?" He asked.

"Si, he must have been dropping off guests for the rental house," Diego answered. "That's a pretty good gig that he has with the management company."

"You think he can afford that expensive toy just bringing the occasional renter to the island?" Pedro asked, his eyes fixed on the retreating yacht.

One eyebrow popped up and Diego's mouth twisted into a cheeky grin, "Don't you believe him?" He clocked the skeptical expression on Pedro's face. The blade-shaped nose, deep-set eyes, and bald head made his brother-in-law look fierce, but he really was a pussy cat at heart.

"Sure, just like I believe in the aluxes," Pedro said, correctly pronouncing the Maya word as alooshes.

"Hey now, watch what you say," Diego playfully shook a finger at Pedro, "Mi abuela, my grandmother, told me the aluxes are real and I believe her," Diego quipped. "As a matter of fact, I have my own personal alux."

"Really. Did your abuela show you how to carve your figurine from stone or clay? And did you drip nine drops of your blood over him so that he knows you are the master?" Pedro quizzed.

"Uh, well, not exactly, I didn't do the blood thing," Diego said. "Is that really a thing you have to do with the aluxes?"

"Si, otherwise he doesn't know who's the boss. And, more importantly, if you don't give your alux daily offerings of food and prayers he will take revenge on you, cause headaches, diarrhea, crop failure, and sick cattle."

"No worries, I don't have crops or cattle."

"That doesn't matter," Pedro leaned a little closer to Diego. "They're mischievous little beings. Do you remember what happened at Chichen Itza just a couple of days before the Elton John concert in 2010?" He asked, in a stage-whisper loud enough to be heard over the roar of the twin diesel motors.

"You mean the concert at the pyramid?"

"Si, that one," Pedro agreed.

"Uh no, not really. What happened?"

"The stage collapsed."

"Verdad?"

"Si, I'm not exaggerating."

"Any one hurt?"

"No, but it created a lot of problems for the organizers."

"What's that got to do with the aluxes?"

"The old people said that it collapsed because the manager didn't perform the ceremony asking for permission," Pedro relaxed back in his captain's chair. "There were permission ceremonies for the previous concerts of Luciano Pavarotti in 1997 and Sarah Brightman in 2009."

"And?"

"No problems at all."

Diego scrutinised Pedro's face, then grunted a laugh, and waved dismissively at his partner, "You don't believe that. It's all superstitious bullshit."

"You're the one who said he has a personal alux. I'm just trying to keep my favourite brother-in-law's ass safe from mythical tricksters."

"I'm your only brother-in-law."

"Which makes you my favourite, ass."

Chapter 17

February 5th Isla Mujeres

Sipping on a tall double-shot latte the Nashville socialite wandered the expansive gardens at the rental house. The grounds were jammed with bougainvillea, oleander, and hibiscus, but not the plant she wanted. She was searching for the inappropriately named Angel's Trumpet. In her view the alternate name, Witches Weeds, was more authentic for the deadly plant.

Her internet research had confirmed that the plant grew abundantly on the island, so she would just have to venture out and locate a source. Worse case scenario she could make do with oleander. She spun around, marching purposefully towards the house. *What the hell was that woman's name?*

"Lupe!" She shouted, picking the first name that came to mind.

The woman's smiling face greeted her, "Yes, madam? How may I help you?"

"I'm taking the golf cart out to explore the island. Where is the key?"

Luz walked to a kitchen drawer, pulled it open and reached inside. "Right here, madam." She said, showing the woman the keys, "This one is for the ignition, this one for the security lock, and this one to access the gas tank when you need more fuel."

"Don't be ridiculous. Find someone to refuel it every day for me." She said snatching the keys from Luz, and strutting to her bedroom.

She stared at her reflection in the mirror. The new hairstyle was good. Short and wispy, with a few very subtle blonde highlights accenting the dark caramel colour. When she returned to Nashville from her alleged spa retreat, she just might keep this style but revert to her natural colour. A new beginning after disposing of her bloodsucking husband. Brown eyes instead of blue stared back at her; costume contacts, that she could easily remove.

There wasn't much she could do about her height, but wearing flats instead of heels would help with the illusion, and she had chosen a wardrobe that was ordinary and cheap. Wearing layers of plain loose clothing, she downplayed the size and shape of her breasts otherwise her darling hubby might actually recognize them. Her only concession to her usual style were several pairs of good quality sandals and slip-ons, but no one would be looking at her feet, they would be drinking, dancing, and partying.

Placing a large brimmed sunhat on her head, and adding the cut-rate sunglasses that she had recently purchased she checked her image again. Good enough for a quick exploratory drive around the island.

Gesturing dismissively at the maid she climbed the stairs to the driveway. At street level, Suzanne stopped and stared at the vivid colour combination of the vehicle. It was painted a dazzling yellow with black trim and had the rental company's bright logo plastered on both sides. It was much too memorable. She had assumed that every golf cart was painted that beige colour, commonly seen on the golf courses.

But, even more annoying than the too-bright colours, the two large gates were blocking her exit.

"Lupe!" She hollered. *Nothing*. She moved to the top of the stairway and bellowed. "Lupe!"

"¿Si, señora?" Luz replied, running up the stairs.

"Gates!" Suzanne said and got into the cart then stared at the petite woman as she awkwardly wrestled the heavy gates open. "And speak English!"

"Yes, of course. I apologise."

Suzanne backed out and headed south, cursing like a longshoreman at the roughness of the unpaved alley.

Bemused, Luz watched the golf cart teeter and rock on its frame as the woman ignorantly navigated an overgrown pathway that was not meant for vehicles. She closed the gates and called Rodrigo's cell.

"Hola mi amor. Si, I am on my own right now. Madam has gone out for a drive," She said, then added, "Did you know my name is Lupe?"

"Lupe?" Rodrigo questioned, "Why?"

"Because that's what señora Sophia Hayden-Smith calls me," Luz responded with a light laugh.

"That's a mouthful," Rodrigo said. "I'm assuming she doesn't know you refer to her as Her Royal Highness?"

"No, she doesn't," Luz replied with a giggle. "Did I mention that madam informed me the master-suite is much too small."

"Too small! It's larger than our house."

"Claro que sí, but apparently she is accustomed to finer things."

"There are a lot of very rich people in Nashville," Rodrigo acknowledged.

"Si," Luz mused, thinking about the inferior quality of the woman's clothing, "but, she dresses as if she shops at a thrift store."

"People with a lot of money can be eccentric."

"Perhaps that's the reason," She said, "And then this morning I saw her carefully examining all the plants in the garden. Not the sort of behaviour I expected from someone who doesn't like to get her hands dirty."

"Odd," Rodrigo agreed, "or maybe she has a big garden and was looking for new ideas."

"That could be, but I am certain she would have gardeners. She doesn't do anything that could damage her precious manicure. She insisted that I open the gates, while she waited impatiently in the golf cart," Luz said. "If it had a horn, she would have been leaning on it to hurry me up."

"Mi amor, if this woman is too difficult you can always quit. You have a solid reputation. You could find another job easily," Rodrigo said, "I don't like you being treated so badly."

"No, no. Don't worry," Luz reassured Rodrigo, "She is only here for two weeks, and I get paid very well to put up with the outrageous demands of the clients."

"Are you sure?"

"I'm certain. It's how we can afford to send our niños to a better school," Luz reassured Rodrigo. "Oh, and before I forget, Her Royal Highness demands that someone top up the tank on the golf cart, every day. Could you do that for me?"

"Si, of course. I'll bring a can of gas to the house when I'm finished working."

"Te quiero, I love you." She air-kissed the phone and ended the call. "Time to earn my money," she said, heading to the bedroom to change the linens even though the woman had only been here one night. She had specified in her rental agreement that she required fresh sheets and fresh towels every day. Madre de Dios.

Luz bent and picked up a pair of red loafers on the floor, planning to place them in the custom-made shoe rack inside the walk-in closets. One shoe escaped from her fingers and fell to the floor, revealing a red sole with a scrawled Louboutin signature. Never in her lifetime would Luz have the money for these shoes, but she recognized them from the ads in the gossip magazines.

She carefully placed the shoes in the built-in shoe rack.

Chapter 18

February 5th Isla Mujeres

Brandon Forbes ambled outside. He raised his arms overhead feeling his joints pop, releasing the tension in his shoulders. This was going to be a great week. The best part was being a long way away from that pinched-face bitch he was married to: Suzanne.

Last night had been comfortable sharing the multi-bedroom beach house with some of the Nashville entertainers who were part of the music festival. He and a few of the other musicians had got an early start on making music and swigging good booze.

Today there were two events scheduled, but he wasn't officially required to be at either of them. One at the *Little Yellow School House* where several of the musicians were going to entertain the students. The kids were cooking lunch for everyone but he was giving that one a pass; he just wasn't a kid-person.

Twisted Isla

The other event was according to his room-
mates later in the afternoon at a beach club *El
Pescadore*, located somewhere along this street. He
might drop in and see what was going on,
assuming he wasn't otherwise occupied.

He wandered over to the golf cart, the one
assigned for his use. He liked the idea of having his
own transportation, to be able to zip around the
island, or come back when he needed a bit of
privacy with whatever sweet young thing that he
had with him.

Stepping into the cart he planted his butt on
the vinyl covered seat, then turned the key, and
experimentally pushed the gas pedal. The brake
released as soon as he hit the gas, and the little
vehicle lurched forward with a jerky bounce. He
stomped the brake pedal and stopped just shy of
bashing into the entrance stairway.

*Alright then, that was fun. Now, where's
reverse?*

Brandon looked down and noticed a large
dial with a black plastic indicator pointing at words
too faded to read.

If it's in forward gear, he reasoned, *then
moving the pointer to the opposite side should give
me reverse. Maybe.*

He turned the dial and gingerly pushed on the gas pedal. *Success.* The cart moved backwards. He backed up, turned around, drove to the edge of the driveway and looked both directions hoping for a clue as to which way he should go. Yesterday when Michelle had dropped him off at the house they had been chatting and he hadn't paid any notice to his surroundings.

Left, he decided and turned the steering wheel. It was a small island and he wasn't likely to get lost - for too long.

A couple of minutes later the light vehicle jolted up and banged down. "Shit, goddamn speed bumps." He looked ahead and seeing a series of the hard, black ribs bolted onto the pavement; a few were marked with bright yellow strips, others just lay there, dark and ominous, like a crocodile waiting for its prey. Easing up on his speed, he resumed driving.

Passing a succession of homes, an attractive hotel, and then a place to swim with the dolphins, Brandon arrived at a dead-end turnaround. To his left was a large, expensive looking compound with two or three houses barricaded behind an impressive gate. Straight ahead was a tangle of mangroves hiding the view of the ocean and to his right was a tiny bar, *La Palapa del Capitan*, tucked into the edge of the jungle beside a muddy road. He checked his phone.

Eleven in the morning was a good time to have his first beer of the day. Okay, technically speaking not his first, first. But definitely his first since breakfast. If you had a creative mind there could be many firsts during a day.

He stomped on the brake pedal to engage the park mode, then stepped out of the cart and sauntered towards the bar. Twenty minutes later he waved goodbye to the proprietor and headed back the way he had come. According to the bar owner he needed to drive to the roundabout with the statue of a fisherman, and then either turn left and left again to find his way to el centro, or drive straight to tour the entire island via Punta Sur.

The man had assured him, even if he got lost, he could find his way back to his accommodation in Sac Bajo by always keeping the ocean on his right-hand side while driving.

Stifling a beer flavoured belch Brandon started the motor and turned around, heading in what he assumed was a southerly direction. An interesting collection of houses painted combinations of pink, orange, blue, yellow, green and white flowed past.

The homes were interspersed beach clubs, offering day-passes for visitors to spend the day eating and drinking at their establishment. Zama's Beach Club had a signboard advertising a festival event scheduled for the next day. Then a short distance later he passed the house where he was staying.

"That's convenient. I can stagger from the house to Zama's and stagger back. No need to drive." He said, then repeated the name of the house a few times. Even if he was falling-down drunk, he would still be able to recognize it - hopefully.

He slowed to read a sign, with a painting of sea turtles, posted at the end of a narrow lane advertised it as the *Tortugagranja*. He chewed on his bottom lip, and mulled that one around. The turtle farm that's what it was; Michelle had mentioned it. This was where thousands of turtle eggs were hatched out and then the babies were released into the ocean. It was a long running conservation program implemented to save the sea turtles from predators; dogs, birds, and humans.

It might be worth a look, but on second thought he remembered her saying that the turtle nesting season didn't start until late May. So, forget that.

"Watch out!" Shouted an angry female voice.

Startled, Brandon snapped his head towards the noise, as another golf cart sped around him. He only saw the back of the driver's head and shoulders. The person was wearing a large floppy hat; she was probably the woman who had shouted at him.

Noticing that he was straddling the centre line, as faint and faded as it was, he turned the steering wheel and inched back into his lane.

"I'm getting thirsty and gotta find me another bar. This sight-seeing stuff is a waste of valuable drinking time," He depressed the gas pedal and sped south towards the traffic circle, then slowed indecisively until he noticed a brightly painted sign pointing straight ahead.

"*The Joint*, that's the one the guys were talking about last night. Good food, good music, cold beer, and plenty of pretty women. My type of place."

Chapter 19

February 5th Isla Mujeres

Carrying a heavy tray loaded with dirty dishes and empty glasses Jessica danced sideways, sucked in her non-existent tummy and dodged past a big group of customers at the *Loco Lobo Restaurant*. The place was jammed. Ten people were crammed around a table designed for six. Every seat both inside and out on the street were occupied. Chatter and laughter ricocheted off the hard-surfaced floors and walls, spilling out onto Hidalgo Avenue. Music flowed. Peppy tunes about sun, sand, sex and alcohol cranked up the energy level in the restaurant.

The Island Time Music Festival had started the day before and the island was jammed with musicians and tourists. Her blood sizzled with energy. This was, in her opinion, one of the best times of the year to be on the island.

Carlos and Yasmin had suggested that the staff dress country and everyone had joined in, donning hats, neck bandanas, denim shorts, and gingham shirts in their own version of what country folks wore.

Jessica had discovered a pair of hand-tooled cowboy boots at a specialty store in Cancun that looked great, but they were destroying her feet. She needed to find five minutes to switch back to her usual footwear before she was crippled with pain and blisters.

"Can we get more drinks?" Hollered a young guy wearing a trendy and fashionably battered Stetson.

"Absolutely handsome," She grinned at the guy whom she mentally labeled as Cowboy Dude, and said, "Give me two minutes to empty my tray."

Scooching to the side to allow other servers access to the bar, Jessica rapidly off-loaded the glassware and dishes into the bussing pans ensuring that she picked out the cutlery before dumping the remaining food scraps into the garbage. She knew it exasperated Carlos when he would randomly check the garbage cans and find an assortment of knives, spoons and forks. Busy staff sometimes took shortcuts and dumped the contents of their trays without sorting the utensils from the uneaten food.

"Hey, Jess, have you used any of your free passes for the music fest yet?" Asked the assistant bartender, Isabela.

Jessica skimmed a hurried glimpse at Isabela, "Not yet," She said, shaking her head.

"That's too bad. The street party at *Tiny Gecko's* last night was freaking awesome."

"I heard the music was great and that the *Drink Flamingo Project* were hilarious."

"Yes, it was tons of fun last night," Isabela said, "Are you using tonight's pass?"

The hopeful tone in Isabela's voice caused Jessica to look up, "No, I'm working until closing time. Do you want it? It starts at five o'clock at the *El Pesacadore* beach club."

"Yes, please! I'm off in thirty minutes. That gives me just enough time to dash home and change before the event."

Wiping down her tray Jessica smiled at Isabela, "I'm sure Mike would like someone to put the pass to good use."

"Are you sure he won't mind?"

"I explained when he gave them to me, that I wouldn't be able to attend every event. He understood, mostly." Jessica said with a little self-conscious lift of one shoulder. "I've switched shifts with Caitlin on Friday so that I can go to the *Big Daddy's Beach Party*."

"That's awesome. Thank you so much, Jess," Isabela said.

"No worries, remind me before you leave. I'll give you the ticket," Jessica replied, wiping down the now empty tray and hurrying back to table fifteen, "Thanks for waiting folks," She cranked up the wattage and beamed at the guy in the battered hat, "What can I get you, handsome?"

"How about …" Cowboy Dude flinched and glared crossly at the red-head sitting beside him. "What?" He snapped.

Jessica bit down on a smirk. He'd been giving Jessica's body the once-over and Cranky Red-head had retaliated, elbowing him sharply in the ribs.

"You're with me. Remember?"

"I. Know." He peevishly replied. Avoiding eye-contact with both Jessica and the red-head, Cowboy Dude raised his voice to be heard over the babble of multiple conversations and made a circular motion with his finger, "Same again for everyone?"

A chorus of agreement rippled around the table, and Jessica made a quick notation, including a frozen margarita with salt for Cranky Red-head.

She flashed her orthodontically-perfect smile at the group, "I'll be right back with your orders." Spinning on the balls of her feet, she executed a graceful pirouette. Her heavy blonde plait swayed, then settled between her shoulder blades. Hopefully Cowboy Dude had protected his ribs when he snuck a look at her jazzy exit.

"How are you holding up Yassy?" Jessica asked. Yasmin had abandoned her invoice checking and bill-paying duties to assist the bartenders.

"I'm good. I haven't done this for awhile, but I haven't forgotten how." Yasmin answered.

"Kind of like riding a bicycle, you never forget," Isabela chirped.

Jessica chuckled in agreement, and added her order to the line-up. "Same again, please."

"What can I do to help?" Carlos asked.

Jessica noticed that he had rolled the sleeves on his white linen shirt half-way back to his elbows, exposing his muscular forearms and his Rolex watch. Yasmin had once confided that she thought he looked sexy, very sexy when he did that.

Jessica had to admit, Carlos was a smoking hot guy. "Lookin' good boss," She winked at her friend. "Could you refill our supplies?" She flapped a hand at the shelves containing napkins, straws, lime slices, cherries, and the silly little paper umbrellas for the foo-foo drinks. "We're running low."

"Got it," He said, "Anything else?"

"Check on the food-runners. Make sure they're keeping up with the orders coming out of the kitchen."

"Already did that," Jessica heard Carlos say as the gorgeous voice of Maggie Rose cut through the background clatter of the restaurant.

Yeah, it's you I was waiting for, and I never ever saw you coming. Yeah, I need you forevermore, and I never wanna see you go.

"Wow! Her voice gives me goose bumps," Jessica said rubbing her bare arms.

"Her voice is stunning," Agreed Carlos.

"I'll get to see her perform on Friday night at *Big Daddy's*. I'm so excited," Jessica piled the new drink order on her tray and headed back to Cowboy Dude and Cranky Red-head.

Chapter 20

February 5th Isla Mujeres

There was a brief afternoon lull at the *Loco Lobo*, and Carlos remembered his truck was running on fumes. Earlier, his head chef had sent him on an emergency run to Chedraui to buy more produce, in particular he needed more of the ingredients required for their popular guacamole.

The annoying low-gas alarm, had pinged incessantly on the return trip from Chedraui back to the restaurant. If he didn't refill the tank now, getting home after the restaurant closed could be a gamble. If they ran out of gas on the way home it wouldn't be a huge deal as there were always taxis buzzing around the island, but it would be a big inconvenience to deal with the next day. *Easier to gas up now*.

He checked his pocket, ensuring he had the key fob, and shouted to Yasmin. "Back in a few minutes, we need gas for the truck."

She acknowledged with a brief wave, then continued with restocking the bar in preparation for the next upsurge in customers.

At the Pemex station, Carlos pulled his orange Toyota Tacoma in behind a moto. The attendant was filling a five-gallon jerry can for Rodrigo Hernandez.

"Hola Rodrigo," He said, fist-bumping Rodrigo's hand.

"¿Que pasa hermano?" Rodrigo asked.

"Not much, just getting gas while I have a few minutes," Carlos replied. "Did someone run out of gas?" He asked, nodding at the gas can.

"No, this is to refill the golf cart at one of the rental houses."

Carlos laughed, "We both know most of the carts don't have functioning gas gauges, but I thought the rental companies kept their vehicles topped up."

"Luz asked me to do this as a special favour. The woman that she is currently working for wants the tank topped up. Every. Single. Night." He said with a roll of his eyes.

The pump clicked off, and the gas-jockey replaced the nozzle. Rodrigo handed the him enough to pay for the fuel plus a small propina, a tip.

"Man, I really miss Luz," Carlos said, "but Yasmin insists that we don't need a full-time housekeeper with just the two of us." He sighed, "My slothful bachelor's habits have been wiped out. Yasmin has trained me to make the bed in the morning, wash the dishes after every meal, and take out the trash at night."

Rodrigo laughed at the aggrieved yet comical look on Carlos' face, "Luz understands. Her new job with the rental management company keeps her busy," He said, "but, she preferred working for you. You are family to us, unlike some of the guests that she has had."

"Do the clients give her a bad time?" Carlos asked, the expression in his dark eyes shifted from fake frustration to genuine concern.

"Not very often, although the one who's renting that big white house near Punta Sur is very rude. Luz insists she can deal with her." Rodrigo lifted his shoulders in a frustrated motion, "I don't like the situation, but she wants the money for our kids' education."

"Still, I'm sorry to hear she is being treated badly," Carlos said.

"No worries, todo bien," Rodrigo continued, "you know Luz, she can usually find something to laugh about, no matter what. This morning Luz said the señora was rooting around in the garden and carefully examining every plant, but yet she didn't want to get her delicate little hands dirty by opening the gates." He chuckled, "And she dresses cheaply but is paying a fortune for a two-week rental of a five-bedroom house, just for one person."

Carlos shook his head, "Rich people. They live in an alternate universe."

Rodrigo checked a message on his phone, then pocketed it, and hopped onto his moto. He lifted the plastic can, balancing it in front of him on the gas tank of his moto. "Got to go. Her Royal Highness is back from her ride around the island. Luz wants me to fill up the cart, and then give her a ride home from work."

"She not on call 24-7?" Carlos asked, only half-joking.

"Apparently the renter told Luz she could leave as soon as the tank was re-filled," Rodrigo said. "I want to get her out of there before the woman changes her mind."

"Hasta luego, give my love to Luz."

Rodrigo waved goodbye and drove quickly to the south end of the island, where he turned and bumped along a rutted dirt lane until he came to a large modern house. He stopped and shut off the engine, made sure the moto was balanced on the kickstand, then slung his leg over the seat and stood on the ground. He hefted the gas can in one fist, and opened the smaller pedestrian gate with his other hand.

Setting the container beside the golf cart, Rodrigo checked the seat and confirmed was locked in place as a deterrent against fuel theft. This tactic was an ineffective deterrent in most cases. Many of the thieves merely crawled underneath the frame, twisted off the gas cap, and siphoned the liquid out of the tank. The secondary step of placing a larger PVC drain cover on top of the cap usually slowed down the thieves but sometimes they just pried up the seat with a crowbar to access the tank.

Luz would know where the key was kept. He descended the stairs to the main living area and peaked around the corner. He didn't want to accidentally barge in on the guest in case she was sunbathing by the pool, with or without a suit.

"Luz?" He softly called, "Luz?"

"Who the hell are you?" Bellowed a rail-thin woman.

"Lo siento señora. Soy el esposo de Luz." This must be the infamous Sophia Hayden-Smith that Luz had told him about. She was dressed in shorts, a loose blouse, sandals, and carrying a woven beach bag with some type of plant poking out of the top.

"Speak English or I'll call the police." Sophia Hayden-Smith said, as she set the bag down behind the white sofa.

"I'm sorry to startle you, lady. I'm the husband of Luz."

"Who the hell is Luz?"

"Your maid," Rodrigo replied, tightening his jaw.

"Her name is Lupe!"

"No, her name is Luz." He replied evenly, then continued, "I have gas for your vehicle but I need the keys to access the tank."

"Stay there!" Hayden-Smith, pointed a thin finger at the spot where Rodrigo stood. "Lupe, come here! There's a man here who says he's your husband."

Luz appeared from a second set of stairs, the inside access for the upper floors. "Si, madam,

Rodrigo is my husband," She quickly interjected. "You asked me to ensure that your golf cart was refueled every evening, and since he gives me a ride home at the end of my work day, I thought it would be easiest if he brought the gas with him." She hurried through her explanation, trying to prevent señora Hayden-Smith from shouting at her again.

"Fine," Suzanne snapped, "But you should have told me he was coming. I don't like surprises."

"Yes, of course, madam. In the future, I will ensure that I inform you before he arrives." Luz dropped her eyes to the floor. Rodrigo silently stewed watching his wife's submissiveness. This was not like her. She was intelligent and capable. Soft-spoken, but iron-willed.

He soundlessly fumed. *Sophia Hayden-Smith, Her Royal Highness, la maldita perra.*

Chapter 21

February 5th Isla Mujeres

Suzanne, known as Sophia Hayden-Smith to the house staff, turned and stalked into her master-suite, trying to slam the tall heavy door but failing to create the desired effect. The damn thing wouldn't swing fast enough to produce the dramatic vibrations of a door smashing against the frame. The surprise encounter with the maid's husband had been a close call, and she wanted them to think that she was furious. In reality his sudden appearance had alarmed her. She hadn't wanted anyone to see the plants.

Her drive around the island in search of the Witches Weeds had been fruitful. Scarcely noticing the lush tropical scenery or the turquoise ocean, she had driven up and down narrow streets crowded with tiny dwellings, battered cars, beat-up motorcycles, scruffy mongrels, and annoyingly loud children.

Earlier in the morning she had nearly rear-ended a man dawdling along in his golf cart. He had suddenly stopped at the entrance to the *Tortugagranja*, whatever that was.

She had peevishly yelled, watch out. She was about to add dickhead, to her warning, when her brain signalled that she knew those familiar-looking broad shoulders. Brandon.

Ducking her head, she had stomped the accelerator and shot past him. She sped through the round-about, turned a sharp left and felt the two right-side wheels lose contact with the pavement. She intuitively shifted her body-weight to the right. Her quick movement was enough to prevent a rollover, and dropped the tires back to the road. She sped away. Away from Brandon.

Once her pulse had evened out, she continued with her search for the Witches Weeds. Eventually she had discovered a large plant with gorgeous pale orange blossoms and a heavenly scent, growing in chaotic mass of bougainvillea and oleander in front of a ramshackle tin-roofed shack. In her opinion the slovenly owner wouldn't notice a few missing branches.

Wearing a pair latex gloves that she had found under the kitchen sink and wielding a sharp carving-knife from the rental house, she had quickly cut and jammed several blossom-loaded branches into her large canvas carrier. She then carefully stripped off the gloves and stashed them plus the knife in the bag. If the sap of this plant were to touch her skin, it could cause tremors, delusions, and hallucinations.

She had just arrived back at the house and was preparing to wrap the foliage inside an opaque plastic sack, and hide it in the over-sized refrigerator until the meddlesome maid had left. Worse case scenario, she could tape a note on the package for Lupe, or whatever the hell her name was, stating that this was a special herb for her skin and to leave it alone.

Then suddenly the man had poked his head around the corner of the patio, calling his wife's name. For the second time in the same day, she had almost screamed with fright. Almost rear-ending Brandon's golf cart, and now this. Forcefully squelching her reaction, she quickly stashed the bag behind the sofa and confronted the man with a loud and disdainful tone.

The best defense is an offense.

Now, marching into her bedroom she ignored the bag. Hopefully those two dim-wits would just refill the gas tank and leave.

Standing inside the master-suite, Suzanne listened for the sounds of the woman and her spouse leaving. As they climbed the stairway to the parking area, she rushed into the bathroom and opened the small window. She listened intently as they fiddled with the golf cart, presumably adding the fuel to the tank.

Then the maid returned to the kitchen with the keys, "Buenos noches señora. We're leaving now."

Suzanne ignored the woman, listening instead for the sounds of the gate shutting and the moto starting up and driving away.

"Thank God, they're finally gone," She muttered to herself. "Now I can work in peace."

She opened the bedroom door and headed into the kitchen, standing with her hands on her hips she surveyed the many drawers and doors. "Where the hell would someone store a big pot?"

Suzanne had never in her life prepared a meal, or even a snack. Her universe had always included a chef, a butler, maids and other assorted support staff. Irritated she started at one end of the large open-space kitchen and yanked open one of the deep drawers. *Dishes.*

She pulled out a second one. *Cutlery.*

Another was stacked with coffee cups and glassware.

One drawer was filled with tea towels. *Why on earth would someone need that many tea towels? She couldn't remember ever washing or drying a dish in her life. That's why dishwashers were invented. What did she know about how many dish towels were required? She had always had cooks and housekeepers.*

She slammed the drawer shut, then eyed the kitchen. Closest to the stove was a deeper drawer. She pulled that one open. *Pots! Finally.*

Lifting a heavy pot to the cooktop, Suzanne frowned, "How do I turn this damn thing on?" She experimentally turned a knob and heard an electronic clicking sound then flames whooshed in front of her face, "Freaking hell!" She jumped back and glared at the appliance, "Okay, so that's how it works."

Contemplating the empty pot, she suddenly realized that she needed water to create the brew. She lifted it off the burner, noticing the handles were warm even with just those few minutes of sitting on the flame. She set the vessel in the sink and fiddled with the complicated tap until water poured out of the spout.

Lifting the much heavier pot back to the stove was a struggle. She belatedly considered that perhaps she had filled it too full. If she made the brew anywhere near to its potential potency, she would only need about half a cupful to dispatch her *darling* husband. But the branches were large, and it could be a messy operation so it was best to use the biggest container that was available.

Humming to herself, she walked to the sofa and reached behind it to retrieve her bag. She sauntered to the kitchen and plopped the bag on the white counter top. "Music, I need music to help me be creative. And wine. A nice crisp white would be perfect."

Opening the door of the refrigerated wine storage, Suzanne ran her fingers over the dozens of bottles laying horizontal in rows of red, rosé, or white wines. She selected a bottle of Kim Crawford Sauvignon Blanc and twisted off the cap. Lifting a crystal glass from a shelf she poured a generous amount and then placed the open bottle inside the double-doored refrigerator.

"Now, music. Anything but country." Thumbing her iPhone, she located a selection of upbeat songs, "I gotta feeling, by the Black-eyed Peas."

"Tonight's gonna be a good, good night," She sang while pulling on fresh gloves and beginning to add bits of branches, leaves and the flowers to the pot. Everything on the plant was poisonous and the internet had been quite helpful, but it didn't specify exactly how to concoct the poisonous potion. Better to have too much than too little.

Ensuring the tall glass patio doors were fully open and the cooktop's ventilator fan was running at high speed she felt confident that she was safe from the toxic fumes. Leaving the contents to simmer, she strolled around the pool deck admiring the nighttime view of Cancun.

She tipped the glass to her lips and discovered it was empty. Turning on her heel, she headed back to the kitchen. There were many bottles of wine waiting just for her, including two adequate champagnes.

Champagne. Yes, that would be the perfect celebratory beverage for this evening.

Chapter 22

February 6th Isla Mujeres

Feeling a little fuzzy and hungover from consuming an entire bottle of champagne, Suzanne surveyed the *Island Time Music Festival's* webpage, listing the schedule of events. She had previously checked the venues and dates where her gormless mate would be performing, not wanting to arrive on the island too far in advance but with enough time to scoop out the poisonous plants and plan her escape route.

He was scheduled to perform at two of the events on Friday; one was early in the afternoon at *Capitan Dulche's*, and the second was Friday evening at *Big Daddy's* on the beach. That could work to her advantage, he'd be tired and a little drunk. Knowing Brandon, he would start sipping beers early in the morning, be well and truly lubricated by the afternoon event, and then desperately trying to keep his shit together for the evening performance.

Hair of the dog, was his motto; drink more booze when a hangover is threatening to slow you down.

Tapping her fingernail on the kitchen countertop, she pondered the name *Big Daddy's* for a moment. She had recently read something about that location.

"Ah yes, now I remember." She said, "That's the bar that needs extra servers because they are hosting one of the biggest events."

Realizing she was speaking out loud, Suzanne quickly scanned the room looking for the woman Lupe-or-whatever. She didn't see her, but heard water running on the upper level, so the woman was probably cleaning something, or maybe she was just running water so that Suzanne would think she was cleaning something. She wasn't paying Lupe's wages, so not her problem. As long as the woman did her job with preparing food, cleaning the house, and staying out of Suzanne's hair she didn't care how she wasted her time.

"Well, I guess I will do my civic duty and volunteer to be a server," Suzanne mused. "Just to be sure my talented husband doesn't get thirsty. The poor dear will be dehydrated from slobbering over the women in their thong-bikinis."

She opened a door on the Sub-Zero refrigerator, checking that her carefully concocted brew was safely tucked behind an assortment of condiments and salad dressings.

Last night was a bit of a blur, but she vaguely remembered decanting the liquid into three plastic containers, and tossing the mash of leaves, bark and stems over the bank and into the garden. She had swished out the pot and dropped it back in the drawer where she had found it, and staggered off to bed with the remnants of the champagne.

This morning when she finally dragged herself awake, her foot had landed on the empty bottle which rolled underfoot, throwing her off balance. She had nearly landed on her ass. About to scream at Lupe to pick up the damn trash, she remembered that she didn't want the woman to know what she had been doing the previous evening.

Uncharacteristically, she bent over and picked it up. She tossed on a robe and peered out of her room, then quickly scurried towards the garbage can in the pantry. Grimacing she shoved the bottle deep into the can and covered it with other trash. She replaced the lid and holding her arm away from her body she headed straight for the shower.

Now, showered and dressed she realized she was hungry. "Lupe!" She yelled in the general direction of the stairway leading to the upper floor. *What the hell was the woman doing?*

"Yes, madam," a faint reply echoed down the stairs.

"Breakfast," She hollered.

"Of course," Luz said rapidly descending the stairway. "What would you like me to make for you?"

"An assortment of fresh berries, unflavoured yoghurt, one scrambled egg, one slice of unbuttered whole wheat toast, and a no-fat, double-shot latte." Suzanne pointed to the pool patio, "I'll be outside on the deck."

"Certainly. Would you like your coffee first?"

"Of course," Suzanne rolled her eyes not caring if the other woman saw the gesture or not.

Luz inhaled through her mouth, held it to the count of ten, and slowly exhaled out her nose. *Twelve more days of Madam.* She had reassured Rodrigo that she could deal with the client and not to worry about her. But privately she thought that this woman had to be the most ill-mannered and rude guest that she had ever encountered.

Pampering the guests who rented this house was usually not difficult, and the pay was good, but she longed for the warm, and caring atmosphere of working just for Carlos Mendoza. She was happy to do his grocery shopping, cleaning, laundry, anything that he needed during his bachelor hiatus between wife number one, Elena, and his second wife Yasmin.

Luz adored Yasmin, but realized that she wanted to be the *reina*, the queen, of her own home. Maybe when their new restaurant was operational, they would need her to look after their domestic chores again. It would mean a significant drop in wages, but Rodrigo and she could work it out somehow.

In the meantime, Her Royal Highness was waiting for her breakfast. Luz rapidly created a beautiful latte and delivered it to the woman, then scurried back to the kitchen to make her breakfast. It was a simple breakfast that her six-year-old son could have made, but madam apparently didn't do anything for herself.

Pulling open the drawer where the frying pans and pots were stored Luz noticed that the largest pot was on top of the pan that she wanted. She lifted it and set it on the counter, then pulled out the frying pan, and was about to replace the big pot when she smelled a peculiar odor.

Puzzled, she ran a finger around the inside, and sniffed the end of her finger. There was definitely an odd-smelling scum inside the pot, as if something had been boiled in it for a long time.

It smells like overcooked spinach, or perhaps dandelions? How strange, I haven't used this one for weeks.

"Hungry!" Bellowed the woman.

Luz quickly stored the container, scrubbed her hands, and hurried to make madam's breakfast. Lifting a basket of berries from the crisper, she unconsciously rubbed the end of her index finger against the pad of her thumb, trying to soothe the unusual numbness in her finger.

Chapter 23

February 6th Cancun

Valeria Flores fought down the urge to vomit. The office still stunk of death and body fluids. Earlier in the morning the constables, who had the unfortunate task of guarding the location since Rolando's murder, had removed the crime scene tape. One of the constables informed her there was nothing more that the senior detectives needed at the moment, and she was free to clean up. She had swallowed a snort of derision at that statement; as if she was waiting anxiously to scrub away the remains of a person that she knew and liked, well, mostly liked.

There were times when he was a complete pendejo ... but according to her mama, it was bad luck to speak or think ill of the dead. From now on she would only speak of him in a kind manner.

Wielding a bucket, mop, and the ubiquitous cleaning product Fabuloso, she scrubbed and disinfected, tossing the filthy water down the toilet and replenishing with fresh. Over and over. She pushed the death-stained chair outside and rolled it over to the big garbage bins. Someone else could lift it into the bin, or perhaps a scavenger would remove the offensive object.

Physically and emotionally exhausted she slumped into a chair in the office and fingered through the colour-coded file folders, looking for the information on a specific customer. He was a prosperous Cancun businessman who might be interested in keeping Halcón Logistics financially afloat and out of the hands of the creditors, or perhaps he would buy the company from Chab's widow. Valeria, like many of the employees lived from paycheque to paycheque, and the loss of her wages would be devastating to her family. She needed to keep the company operational until someone else could take over.

A piece of plain paper fluttered out from between two folders. She read the name and phone number, then flipped the page over to check for more information. *Nothing.* The page contained only a first name, Bruno, and what looked to be a cell number noted in Rolando's scrawl. She didn't recognize either and set the page aside to continue her search for a white-knight investor.

The almost blank piece of paper tugged at her concentration. This was so out of character for

Rolando; as a man he was an untidy slob, but as a business owner he was obsessively meticulous. Stuffing a piece of paper between two files was just not something he allow himself to do.

"Let's see if this Bruno character will tell me why he was important to you, Rolando," She said as she picked up her phone and keyed in the number. Listening as it rang until the call automatically ended, she said, "No answer and no way to leave a message," She placed the paper on the desk, tapping the edge with her fingernail. Maybe she should mention the name and phone number to the policeman with the Basset-hound face, Detective Cervera, as a conciliatory action for withholding information when they first questioned her. It was probably nothing, but perhaps it could buy her a little forgiveness from the *policía*.

"That was my new bestie Valeria Flores," Detective Cervera said as he ended the call. "She called to give me a name and phone number that she noticed in her boss's files."

Toledo moved his concentration from the page that he was reading to his partner's face. He rolled his fingers in a please-go-ahead motion, "And?"

"No idea. But she seemed to think it might interest us," Cervera said, as he keyed in the number.

To his surprise a voice answered on the third ring, "Bueno," the man said.

"Hola, is this Bruno?" Cervera asked, at the same moment a mobile radio squawked. The dispatcher was calling a patrol car to respond to a traffic accident.

Cervera made a face, "Well, that was very rude, he hung up on me," Cervera said as he tried the number again, but it rang until it disconnected. "No answer."

"He's probably already pulled the battery and tossed the phone," said Toledo, referring to the habit of career criminals buying cheap phones, using them once or twice, and destroying the device so that it couldn't be tracked.

"Si," Cervera said, "I'll put this number in the file for Rolando Chab López. It could be a clue, or it could just be a random notation on a piece of paper."

"So, you're saying you're clueless?"

Chapter 24

February 6th Isla Mujeres

"How the hell did the policía get my number?" Bruno Torres muttered. He had ignored an earlier call from an unknown number, but after two calls in rapid succession his curiosity had gotten the better of him.

The instant that he had heard the distinctive sound of a police mobile in the background, he instinctively dropped the phone on the ground and destroyed it.

He bent over and retrieved the splintered carcass of the cell phone. A heavy concrete building block dropped from knee height had thoroughly squashed the device, rendering it useless. He skimmed the battery into the mangroves swamp, located across the street from the new hotel project in Sac Bajo.

The only person who had this number was Rolando Chab and he knew for certain the man was dead, because he had shot him in the head. Chab's rapidly cooling body hadn't even twitched while he searched the man's office and warehouse and carted away the windfall from the larger safe.

He felt a momentary twinge of guilt for not divvying up the bonus loot with his compañeros. They were paid their agreed upon share from the gas station robbery, but nothing more. As far as he knew they had no idea that he had taken all of the extra swag.

That still didn't answer the troublesome question of who knew about this phone number, and his name. He huffed out his cheeks, watching as one of his crew furtively glanced over at him. Intrigued, Bruno pointed to a secluded area behind the tool bodega, then ambled in that direction.

Chapter 25

February 6th Isla Mujeres

Another bar, another untouched drink, and another afternoon feeling like a love-struck fool.

Mike Lyons rocked up on his toes for the umpteenth time, searching the crowd at *Zama's Beach Club*. His eyes scanned the multi-level facility, hoping to spot Jessica. She had warned him that because of work she couldn't attend many of the events. *A guy could hope. Couldn't he?*

But, after hearing stories about her various escapades this was probably the last place on the island that she wanted to be; at *Zama's*, in a noisy crowd, and loud music.

The previous February, Jessica was the maid-of-honor at the wedding of Yasmin and Carlos. Eschewing a formal head-table arrangement for the reception the wedding party members had been scattered throughout the crowd. Jessica and her date were seated with her parents Anne and Gord Sanderson, her two reportedly bear-sized and protective brothers Matt and Jake, plus her aunt Pattie Packard.

A gunman, who was later identified as a cartel hitman, had shot at Jessica but instead hit her aunt. Pattie had leaned forward to speak over the loud music and the bullet intended for Jessica tore through Pattie's shoulder.

Jessica's mother, Anne Sanderson, was an emergency room nurse who reacted instinctively to save her younger sister. A call for the Red Cross ambulance and the doctora, and then a late-night run to the mainland in the *Bruja del Mar*, ensured Pattie received emergency surgery in sufficient time. Over time she had recovered, and rehabilitated her shoulder. According to Jessica, Pattie had just recently returned to work as a nurse.

Jessica hadn't been back to *Zama's* since the incident.

He slumped onto his bar stool, staring reproachfully at his warm, flat beer. *No, she definitely wasn't coming to this event.*

"Is this seat taken?" Drawled a voice.

Mike started to say it was saved for a friend, then he shook his head. "No, go ahead. It's yours." He aimed a friendly smile at the lanky blonde man.

"Much obliged," The man said, tapping the brim of his well-worn cowboy hat with a finger. "Brandon Forbes," He added sticking out his hand.

The pretentious mannerism of the city-dude pretending to be a good ole country boy amused Mike. He clasped the hand and gave it a shake, applying a firm pressure but not the mashing grip of an alpha male trying to establish who had the biggest willy. He didn't need to play that game. "Mike Lyons, pleased to meet you."

"Where y'all from?"

"Canada. You?" Mike replied. Over the years he had discovered that answering in an uncomplicated manner was easier than trying to describe exactly where he lived in Canada. Non-Canadians rarely recognized the names of any cities other than the three largest; Vancouver, Toronto and Montreal. The popular belief seemed to be everything else was big, probably uninhabited, and definitely a snow-covered wasteland.

"Nashville. I'm singing at some of the events."

"I'm impressed," Mike said sincerely, "are you preforming at this one?"

"Nope, I have two tomorrow, back-to-back." Forbes raised two fingers to his mouth and blew a short, shrill tone. When the bartender lifted his head to look, he said, "Corona con limon, por favor."

"That's rough," Mike empathised.

"Yes sir, sand, sun, and bikinis all damn day."

"Tough gig," Mike laughed. "So, I guess that means you playing at *Big Daddy*'s tomorrow evening?"

"Yep, that's one of the places. Are you going?" Dropping the plastic tokens on the bar, plus a gratuity, Brandon picked up his beer and turned on his stool so that his back rested against the bar and his view was of the crowd.

"Yes, I bought the all-access pass."

"Great, then I'll probably see you there," Brandon replied, without making eye contact. "Oooh, that's nice."

Mike turned around to look at whatever had caught the musician eye; a stacked red-head in a thong bikini. Her top was two star-shaped pieces of cloth held up by string-width straps. The fabric struggled to cover her nipples. "Yes, it is," he agreed, "dangerously nice."

"I believe I'll go and introduce myself," Brandon said, once again touching the rim of his hat, western-style. "Y'all have a good day now."

Amused, Mike's eyes tracked Brandon as he confidently approached the scantily-clad woman and with the ease of a well-trained cutting horse edged her away from her friends. *Obviously, not his first rodeo.*

Pushing his stale beer aside, Mike ordered a fresh one from the bartender, then turned around to watch the musicians. Kellie Pickler was currently on stage, entertaining the mob with great tunes and her infectious sense of humour. The crowd loved her.

To his left, he overheard snatches of conservation between a young woman and a group of friends. She was bragging how she had been stopped four times in one day for drinking and driving. Each time she had lifted her crop-top and flashed the young male cop with her bare breasts. She laughingly told her audience that she had gotten away without paying any fines. She then proceeded to give the bartenders and nearby patrons an eye-popping look at her enormous, and unnaturally perky breasts.

Mike chuckled. He was pretty sure the policía had enjoyed the experience. They had probably radioed other checkpoints with a description of the golf cart and the woman, suggesting they pull her over for their payment.

The woman and her entourage moved towards the dance floor, bumping and grinding against the other patrons until a small space was created for them. Watching the mass of dancers jiggling and bouncing in front of the stage only added to his feelings of loneliness.

Mike heaved a sigh, picked up his drink and edged in the direction of the large swimming pool. He stopped, shook his head. And looked again.

Yep, that couple is definitely having sex in the pool. That took confidence to a whole new level, he gave a wry laugh at his innate bashfulness. He wasn't comfortable with being totally nude in public, much less dropping his laundry and getting' it on for the amusement of the cheering audience. *Whatever floats your boat, buddy.*

He circled around the pool, observing the number of people submerged in the chlorinated water. The turbidity of the pool appeared to be increasing in relation to the bodies per-square-foot-ratio and the accumulation of floating plastic cups. Most of the celebrants were too inebriated to walk and chose to remain where they stood while quaffing their beverages and relieving their bladders.

No amount of chlorine could erase the image from his retina.

Taking one last look at the undulating mass, Mike sighed again and added his second unfinished drink to the pile beside an overflowing garbage can. At least he was sober enough to drive, although, in Mexico, sobriety was a relative thing.

Flexible. Negotiable.

The fine, if you wanted to call it that, depended on how much the police officer wanted in exchange for letting the drivers continue on their way. He patted his pocket, checking that he still had his wallet.

He didn't have impressive surgically-enhanced boobs to pay the bribes.

It would take cash.

Chapter 26

February 7th Cancun

Bruno Torres shifted his weight to the edge of the matrimonial-size hammock, and grimaced when his bare feet touched the cold, concrete floor. He stood, glancing briefly at his girlfriend, Gabriela. Her eyes were closed but he could tell by the rhythm of her breathing, and the tension in her body that she was only pretending to be asleep. *Still angry.*

"Gaby, the brat is awake. Get up and feed him." He ordered as he grabbed his underpants and headed into their tiny bathroom. Leaving the door open he flipped on the light, squared his feet to the open toilet and casually splashed his stream in the general direction of the bowl.

Reaching inside the small concrete cubicle, he turned on the shower. They didn't have the luxury of a hot water heater, and leaving the shower running in hopes that it would warm up was an expensive waste. It was February. The water was going to be cold, freaking cold, no matter how long he let it run.

He inhaled and quickly stepped inside. "Mierda!" He yelled, rapidly soaping his body. In less than four minutes he was washed, rinsed and done. He pulled a thin towel off the hook, and tried to rub some warmth back into his body. Running his palm over his face and neck, Torres decided that he didn't need to shave yet. Shaving was at most a bi-monthly task, not a daily chore. His Mayan ancestors had given him sparse facial hair and a smooth hairless chest.

He pulled on his shredded jeans, ripped and worn by hauling heavy materials on the jobsite and brushing against rough concrete. He added a black t-shirt and scuffed work boots then sauntered the few steps to the small alcove where Gaby sat with the baby, "Where's my coffee?" He demanded.

She sullenly turned her head away, shifted her son to her hip, and stood. She reached for the coffee carafe, poured the liquid then pushed the cup towards him.

He regarded her with a smirk, "You might want to improve your attitude or find someplace else to raise your little bastard."

Gaby turned towards him, "You hit me," One brown eye glittered at him. The skin around the closed eye was a puffy and impressive combination of purple, black, and red. She held a piece of paper towel up to her bottom lip, dabbing the blood welling up from the unhealed split.

"And I have told you before, keep the hell away from my stuff," Torres said. "You're just too stupid to learn," He drained the coffee, tossed his empty cup into the metal sink with a loud clang, and smiled when he saw her flinch.

"I'll be home late. Do. Not. Touch. My. Stuff," He said. "You got that?"

"Si," Gabriela replied. Her eyes aimed at the kitchen table, she refused to meet his glare.

"Shhh, quiet mi amor," Gabriela Ordaz whispered to her son. She offered him the bottle again, smiling lopsidedly as his chubby fists joined hers to hold the weight. The cut on her bottom lip made smiling difficult, "How did this happen?" She asked the infant. "I'm only seventeen, how did my life go so horribly wrong?"

She removed the bottle from her son's mouth, and placed him on her shoulder, gently rubbing his back until he erupted with a burp. "Okay, back to bed for you. Mama has things to do." She placed the drowsy infant in his basket, tucking his blanket securely around his tiny form.

Tears tracked down her face as she toyed with her phone, wondering if her parents would forgive her for disobeying them. For getting pregnant with a Cancun bad-boy, Bruno Torres. For ignoring their warnings that he was worthless, not good enough for their only daughter. For being rude and insolent and telling them to mind their own business, that she was old enough to make her own decisions after all she had recently had her quinceañera. She was a woman now.

"I am so, so sorry, Mami. I was wrong, so very wrong," She murmured to herself.

Late last night she had made another terrible mistake. Bruno had been very secretive, quietly moving items from the trunk of his battered Nissan into their tiny apartment. Their only closet now contained stacks of cash, and drugs, and two guns. She was terrified.

Without thinking she had confronted him, asking questions. "What have you done? Where did this stuff come from? Where's your truck? Did someone steal it? Why are you driving that terrible old Nissan?"

Wordlessly he had back-handed her, then when she wouldn't stop shouting at him, he had punched her twice in the face. "Shut. Up." Was all he said.

For the first time in her life, she was afraid. Scared to the bone terrified. Afraid for her son and herself. Bruno had undergone a rapid change since her pregnancy. When she refused to party with him and his friends, getting high on drugs and alcohol for fear of damaging the baby he had become physically and verbally abusive to her, then he accused her of cheating on him while he was a work. He denied that he was the father of baby Emiliano, but she knew he was. She had only ever been with him, no other man. He was her first and her only.

She tentatively tapped her phone, holding her breath until the familiar voice answered.

"Bueno."

She exhaled, "Mama, it's me, Gaby," and she began to sob.

Torres impatiently flashed his ticket at the ferry attendant, then angrily strode towards the inspection station leading to the boarding lineup. The green light blinked on for him, letting him bypass the secondary inspection of his backpack.

He laughed at the lame procedure; as if he was going to smuggle a few grams of drugs onto the island. He had a more lucrative arrangement with Damian Hau, hiring him and his boat to transport larger quantities. Hau was an independent contractor for a large company, who provided a private service to and from Isla Mujeres for wealthy clients. Any business between the two of them was strictly cash, and that went directly into Hau's pocket.

But now, he had a problem. A big problem. Gaby. She had snooped through his things that he had stashed in their apartment. Stupid bitch. If she blabbed and his crew discovered that he was holding out on them ... well, the situation could get awkward. It was time to cut and run. He had money and a change would be good. He was bored with her. Bored with his job. And bored with his life.

He would wait one more day, until Saturday, payday for workers in Mexico. That would give him a few more pesos for his traveling money. But what should he do about his truck? Leave it? Or take it?

Take it, he decided. After they were paid, he would drive the truck off the island, stop at the house, load up his stuff, and disappear.

Chapter 27

February 7th Cancun

Gaby paced inside the tiny apartment, alternating between peering out the window and listening for noises. She was terrified that Bruno would return and catch her, suitcase packed and ready to go. She was certain he didn't love her anymore, or if he had ever loved her, but his ego wouldn't allow her to leave him.

Three hours after her phone call, Gaby saw her papa's old, sun-faded pickup wheeze to a stop in front of the multi-story building, just off Avenida Bonampak.

The trip from their hometown of Valladolid would have been quicker if her papa, José Ordaz, could have driven on the cuota, the toll-roads, but she knew he couldn't afford the expensive charges and had to drive on the libre, the free road. From Valladolid the route traveled through ten picturesque villages each with their reduced speeds, numerous topes, and increased traffic including the dozens of motorbike-taxis swarming the streets of Leona Vicario. When not in a rush it was a pleasant, interesting drive, but today, she had just wanted her papa to get here as quickly as possible.

The thought had briefly crossed her mind to ask her father to drive the cuota. She could take some of the money that Bruno had stashed in the closet to reimburse him for the expensive tolls, but she hadn't. She knew that was stupid and dangerous.

And now her papa was here.

Gaby carefully balanced Emiliano in one arm, opened the door and stepped into a hallway that reeked of humanity and poverty. The elevator was broken, again. She would have to drag her suitcase down four flights of stairs, while carrying the baby. A foot scuffed. She froze.

"Gabriela?" José Ordaz, called as his head appeared in the staircase."

"Papa!"

"Madre de Dios! Gabriela, what has he done to you?" He held her at arms length; his worried eyes swept over her face.

"It's nothing, Papa. Let's go. Please."

"Wait, let me look at my new grandson," He said, gently lifting the blanket away from the baby's face. "He's very handsome. What's his name?"

"Emiliano," She shifted her weight, glancing nervously up and down the hallway.

"You named him for me?" The pride in her father's voice was unmistakeable. He obviously still loved her even though they had been estranged for almost eighteen months, ever since she had run away with Bruno.

"Si Papa, José Emiliano, just like you. Now please, we have to go." She turned to lock the door, hopefully for the last time then scurried with her head down towards the stairway.

He followed, dragging her wheeled-suitcase.

Once they were clear of the roaring, hotchpotch of the Cancun traffic, Ordaz turned his head slightly to look at his daughter, "Gabriela, mi amor, tell me. What happened?"

"I'm so sorry that I was disrespectful to you and Mama. You're right. Bruno is not a good person." She said, then stumbled to a halt. She cautiously dabbed at her damaged face, wiping her tears with the corner of her son's blanket.

"That's the past. Tell me."

Accompanied by the steady thrum of the tires against the pavement, she stared out the window, not seeing the tangled green blur of jungle, only seeing the rage on Bruno's face. She told her dad everything; the abuse, the drugs, the money, and the guns.

"Guns! Inside our apartment, with my baby," She wailed.

José listened in silence. His hands gripped the steering wheel until his knuckles gleamed white against his coffee-coloured skin. A muscle ticked in his jaw. He waited until she fell silent, then reached out one hand and grasped hers, squeezing it affectionately. "Don't worry, mi amor, you are safe now."

"Gracias, Papi," Her face crumpled. Fresh tears rolled down her cheeks and dripped onto her baby. "I love you, so much," She said, wiping her face.

"And I love you, and our little Emiliano," He said, giving her a wink. A comfortable silence settled over them for a few minutes.

"I do have a question though," He said breaking the silence.

"Okay."

"Did you hear about the recent armed robbery on Isla Mujeres?"

Gaby's lips pursed in a pout; she shook her head, "No papi," She didn't understand his question. Her world consisted of caring for her baby. She didn't know, nor care about, what was happening on an island that she had never seen.

"I read about it in the papers. Did Bruno ever mention it?"

"I don't think so."

"But you said he works on the island, right?"

"Si, in construction. But what does that have to do with the robbery?"

"A black truck, just like Bruno's was seen at the Pemex gas station around the time of the robbery." He peered at her, as if he expected her to grasp the significance of this piece of information.

"Papa, I don't understand what you are trying to tell me."

"Do you think that might be where the money and drugs came from?" He briefly looked her way, then back to the road ahead.

She blinked, stared at the dashboard, shook her head and then looked at her dad, "Bruno? No, that's not possible."

"Why not?"

"He's Emiliano's papa," She said defensively as she hugged her baby tighter. "I would've known."

"Gabriela, look in the mirror. We're talking about the same man who beat you severely last night," Ordaz said, his voice was kind, but firm. "People are often not what they seem to be."

She studied her battered face in the side mirror, "He hasn't been driving his truck for more than a week," She admitted, "I thought he might've sold it and not told me. He doesn't tell me anything." She heard the whine in her voice, sounding helpless and weak. *What had happened to her confidence?*

"Perhaps he sold the truck, or perhaps he has hidden it."

"Maybe."

"Do you know exactly where Bruno works on the island?"

"He mentioned it a few months ago, but I wasn't listening. Emiliano was fretting and colicky," She replied. "I think he said its a big project, a new hotel in an area called Sac Bajo."

"Do you know the placa of the truck?" Her dad asked.

Twisted Isla

Gabriela's face twisted in concentration as she tried to envision the truck and the licence plate, "It ends in 476, lo siento, that's all I remember."

Chapter 28

February 7th Valladolid

José Ordaz placed his coffee cup on the table, propped his chin on his palm, and looked at his wife. He sighed deeply, then scrubbed his work-worn paw over his face. "Is she okay?" He quietly asked, motioning with his head towards where Gabriela and Emiliano were resting.

"Si, the black eye and split lip will heal on their own," Elva replied, laying her hand on his arm. "In time, and with our help, her heart will heal too."

"I think that bastard Torres was involved with the armed robbery on Isla Mujeres," He spat.

Elva pulled her hand back. Her eyebrows furrowed as she looked at her husband, "Why do you think that?"

"Gaby says he has a stash of drugs, money, and guns in their home. She questioned him about it, and that's why he beat her. This time. It has happened before, apparently."

"Oh José, our poor little girl, I wish she had called us sooner," Elva said dabbing her eyes with a tissue.

"Me too," He said, "But at least she's here now." He peered at his slumbering daughter, then said to Elva, "I also read in the papers that a black pickup truck similar to his was seen at the gas station just before the robbery. Plus, he works on Isla."

She cocked her head to one side, "What do you plan to do about it?"

"Do you remember Dante?"

One eyebrow lifted, a knowing smile on her lips, she asked, "Dante Toledo? Our local heartthrob and God's gift to women?"

He snorted, and nodded, "Si, that Dante." With his disturbing resemblance to the actor Tommy Lee Jones, Toledo had been the lothario of the school when Elva and he were students. Once when they had been enjoying a balmy evening in their courtyard, reminiscing about their youth, she admitted to having a teenage crush on Dante. José had quietly thanked God that the other man hadn't noticed her. Elva was his love, his life.

"Yes, of course I remember him. Why?"

171

"He's a detective for the policía in Cancun. I'm going to call him."

"Do you think that's a good idea?"

José understood her reluctance to involve the policía, but Dante was a friend, a person that they grew up with, "Si, I do."

"As you wish," She replied.

José recognized the statement for what it was, her standard answer when she disagreed with him, but not strongly enough to argue the point. He kissed her forehead, then motioned that he was going outside to make the phone call.

Chapter 29

February 7th Cancun

Dante Toledo propped his feet on his desk, and silently regarded his partner.

Feeling the weight of Toledo's stare, Cervera looked up from the paperwork on his desk. "¿Que pasa?" He asked, setting the file that he had been browsing to one side.

"I just had an unusual phone call from an old friend."

Dante's face was twisted in what Cervera referred to as his thinking pose.

"What about?" Cervera picked up his coffee cup, and peered hopefully into it. *Empty. How many was that today?* He tossed it into the trash can. It was probably his turn to brave the daily health lecture from Amelia the barista and get more coffee for both of them. *Soon.*

"The Isla Mujeres gas station robbery."

"What about it?"

"My friend, José, thinks his daughter's ex-boyfriend is involved."

Cervera huffed a laugh, "Or is this just a case of Daddy getting even for the guy upsetting his little princesa?"

"Could be, but he also had some good information."

"I'm listening."

Toledo succinctly relayed the information about the owner of a black pickup, who worked on the nearby island, and had a secret stash at his house in Cancun. And his name was Bruno Torres.

"Another Bruno, or it could be the same one," Cervera leaned forward, propping his forearms on the desk, "Our señora Flores found a phone number for a Bruno in señor Chab's files. Maybe this Bruno is also involved with the murder of Rolando Chab López. Coincidentally guns, money, and drugs are missing from his safe."

Toledo hummed a few bars of, Lawyers, Guns, and Money, "I can't help it," He laughed. "That song always pops into my head when I hear guns and money in the same sentence."

Cervera shook his head, "You're ridiculous." He picked up his cell, and briefly considered climbing the stairs to the rooftop to make the call in private, then dismissed the idea. Toledo and he had already been openly discussing the case in the bull pen, so if there was an informant inside their ranks it was too late to worry about it now. Anyone could have overheard their conversation.

He punched the number for Sergeant Ramirez.

Ramirez answered on the third ring.

"¿Cómo está Ramirez?" He said. "This is Cervera. Okay if I put you on speaker? Detective Toledo is here with me."

"Si, go ahead," He agreed, "Hola Dante."

"Buen día, Ramirez."

"Toledo and I have a case with a possible link to Isla Mujeres," He said, jumping right into the reason for his call.

Ramirez replied. "Which case?"

"A murder of a Cancun trucking company owner. There is a possible tie-in with the January armed robbery on your island."

"What's the connection?" Asked Ramirez.

"Toledo got a tip that the black Dodge Ram crew-cab, seen at the gas station on the night of the robbery, might be hidden on the island at a construction site." Cervera leaned back in his chair and crossed his foot over his opposite knee, relieving some of the pain in his lower back muscles. Beatriz was after him to go see a physiotherapist again, but he wasn't convinced that was the best solution. Losing fifteen kilos of fat would be more helpful, but that wasn't going to happen anytime soon. He enjoyed the delicious meals that she lovingly prepared for him. High in calories. High in fat. And high in flavour. He wasn't going to give up his pleasure of eating without a fight.

"Interesting, but how is that tied in with your murder in Cancun?" Ramirez asked, drawing Cervera's attention back to their telephone conversation.

"The murdered guy had a stockpile of drugs, cash, and guns that are now missing. My source says the ex-boyfriend suddenly brought a similar stash into the house, last night," He replied.

There was a hiss of background noise, and finally Ramirez said, "I still don't get the connection."

"According to our source, the ex-boyfriend also has a day job as a construction worker on the island, and drives a black truck. Gut experience tells me it's the same guy."

"Ah, your famous gut," Ramirez said, teasing Cervera about his knowledgeable guesses that were more often than not correct. "Do you know which project?"

"It's a new hotel in the Sac Bajo area. Do you know it?"

"There are two new hotels in that area. We'll have the patrols check both. Do you have the placa?" He asked, meaning did they know the licence plate number.

"It ends is 476, that's all we have."

"Okay. We'll look for it."

"Gracias," Cervera disconnected the call, and picked up his car keys. "We need to search the house of señor Torres."

Chapter 30

February 7th Cancun

His forearms buttressed by his large belly, Cervera leaned on the front fender of their cruiser and watched the policía truck rock to a dramatic stop in front of the apartment complex on Avenida Bonampak. A spray of gravel peppered the sidewalk, as the tires grabbed the pavement.

"Impressive," He said, giving Toledo a side-eye smirk.

Armed personnel, outfitted in intimidating black uniforms, boots, helmets, and balaclavas rushed to assemble beside the vehicle, then at their leader's signal stormed towards the building. They split into two groups, boots thudding menacingly as they thundered up the stairs to the fourth floor.

Cervera motioned with his head and moved towards the building.

Twisted Isla

A few years ago, a group of local painters had tried to brighten the grim exterior with gigantic murals painted on the end of each building. Now, the paint was peeling, lifting off in large swaths; a combination of summer rainstorms, high humidity, poor-quality paint, and time. Some of the portraits were missing faces, and many of the animals were lacking body parts. Rather than soothing the eye the effect was bizarre, unsettling.

Cervera and Toledo steadily tramped up the odoriferous stairs in the wake of the swarming uniforms. On the fourth floor, Cervera leaned one hand against the wall, "Freaking stairs," He huffed.

Forming up on either side of the door, the team waited for the signal to enter. The leader dropped his fist, and shouted, "Policía!"

The battering ram smashed the insubstantial lock. The door swung open. The invaders shouted overlapping commands, "Armed policía! Get Down. On the floor. Now."

Without taking his eyes off the entrance to the apartment, Toledo retorted, "You're fat and out of shape, Marco."

"Comfortable. Beatriz says I'm comfortable. She says I'm her el osito de peluche. Her teddy bear."

"Fat."

"You do want to be invited again for dinner, correct?" Cervera asked. "Sometime in this century," he added.

"All clear detectives," The leader said, poking his head through the shattered door. Cervera skimmed the man's face, trying to remember his name. *Martinez? Mendez?*

"Beatriz loves me like a son," Toledo countered, as he entered the apartment. Cervera trailed behind. "She'll invite me back."

"An insolent son," Cervera mumbled, his eyes sweeping over the meager belongings of the absentee occupants; a hammock, a small collection of plates, cups and utensils stacked on a plastic drainboard, two chairs, and a table barely big enough for two people. *Tidy but not much to show for someone in the drug business.*

"Detective Cervera, is this what you are looking for?" The leader asked, holding up a sack of what appeared to be cocaine.

"Si, any sign of the guns and cash?" He asked, deliberately not saying guns and money in the same sentence so that Toledo wouldn't be overcome with an irrepressible desire to burst into song. They were already encumbered with two derogatory nicknames, and didn't need to add The Singing Detectives to the list.

"Yes, sir. We've secured two handguns and several bricks of cash."

"Good. Now we have to find the illusive señor Torres, and have a serious chat with him." He said, pushing aside the cheap plastic shower curtain. *No, he's not hiding in here.*

Chapter 31

February 7th Isla Mujeres

Cruising along in the mid-morning sunshine, Jessica steered *Frita Bandita* to the right at the statue of the fisherman turning onto the Sac Bajo Carretera. Today was her day off. Later in the afternoon she would join Mike for the music event at *Big Daddy's* but right now her job was to chauffeur her pooch to his favourite exercise area, the undeveloped space at the end of Sac Bajo. It was an ideal place for him to run, and swim, and roll in disgusting dead things. Doggie heaven.

The land was owned by a massive corporation with plans to develop it into a vacation club or beachfront resort some day in the future. Seemingly afloat on a treacherous base of glutinous clay the land didn't seem a particularly inviting location for sun worshipers. The land base was primarily formed from the decomposing remains of millions of tiny shells and miniscule sea creatures. And mosquitoes! Typically, two days after a rain storm swarms of mosquitoes would hatch out eager to suck the life out of any warm-blooded creature within their territory. Even with the use of repellant, the little buggers would drill through clothing, sticking their needle-like probes into unprotected skin.

Been there. Done that. What a nightmare.

Sac Bajo was also the home range for thousands of the endangered blue crabs. They were skittish, and when disturbed, quickly descended into murky burrows, their comical eyes swivelling fearfully at the end of slender optical stalks.

She had never seen quick-sand, but she was certain this area qualified as a close cousin. On one of the occasions that she had been here with Sparky, she watched in open-mouthed astonishment as the brand-new fire truck was put through its paces in the bog.

Watching it sink, Jessica was sure the only thing that stopped it from disappearing entirely was the length of the vehicle. The rescue of the heavy truck had taken the combined effort of several men, two dump trucks, numerous ropes, and a stack of wooden pallets to break the sucking grip of the chalk-coloured muck. She wondered what story the firefighters had concocted to explain the filthy vehicle to the chief.

As she approached the construction site for a new hotel, she noticed a policía truck. The rooftop lights were lit up with red, blue and white revolving lights; not unusual. First responders in Mexico typically activated the emergency lights anytime the vehicles were motion. It seemed to be more of a statement, than a safety requirement.

Mildly curious about what was going on, she glanced in her rear-view mirror, checking for following traffic then pulled to the right and stopped.

A group of uniformed personal seemed to be searching the storage areas and bodegas. Suddenly a burst of excited chatter broke out, as a constable pointed eagerly at a large storage shed tucked behind the main building. Another man drew his pistol and flung open the door to the building. Judging by the peaked cap and epaulets on his shoulders Jessica guessed he was the jefe, the boss.

He appeared to be thrilled by the discovery, but all she could see was the tailgate of a black pickup. The officer bent to check the licence plate, then checked something on his phone and fist-pumped the air.

"I guess he found what they were looking for," She commented to Sparky, then pushed on the accelerator and headed towards their destination.

Parking off to one side at the turnaround, she waved at the proprietors Pedro and Marlena of *La Palapa del Capitan* and carefully helped Sparky skirt past the wicked edge of the razor-wire fencing to gain access to one of the last wild areas on the island. The ugly wire had recently been installed as solution to a volatile ownership dispute.

"Oh man. He's going to need a bath when we get home," She said, her eyes tracking Sparky as he bounded joyously across the watery muck. He resembled a large rabbit, with floppy ears.

A tall white crane squawked in protest and lifted off, flew a few wingbeats, then settled at a new location with an irritate shake of his impressive feathers.

"Don't get lost," Jessica shouted after her disappearing pooch, "We're going out tonight with Mike Lyons."

"You like him, right?" She asked.

Sparky was too busy to respond.

"I'll take that as a yes."

Chapter 32

February 7th Isla Mujeres

Jessica stood at the entrance to *Big Daddy's* on Rueda Medina, and looked ahead at the lineup of people pressing towards the beach. This was the last big event of the Island Time Music Festival, a celebration that included all the well-known artists. Tomorrow was a windup goodbye party at *Kin Há*, but tonight was the big finale. The organizers probably could have sold double the number of tickets.

She felt badly that due to her work schedule she hadn't been able to take full advantage of the expensive gift from Mike Lyons. Tonight, she planned to have fun, enjoy the music, and his company.

Laughter. Cheers. Servers weaving through the crowd with drinks and snacks. It looked like pandemonium, but her experienced eye told her the waitstaff had it under control, for the moment.

She arrived at the admission desk, and showed her all-access pass to the volunteers.

"Hi Jessica, how many drink and food tickets do you want to buy?"

"Oh gosh, Sue, I've no idea. Um, give me fifty dollars worth, I guess."

Sue counted out a pile of plastic tokens and handed them to Jessica, in exchange for the cash. "It's standing room only so just squish your way in and have a great time!" She pointed towards the beach, then focused her attention on the next person in line.

"Thanks." Glancing down at Sparky, Jessica realized that this wasn't the best place to bring him. Compared to humans, dogs have super-sensitive hearing, and because he was short, he might not be visible to the busy servers. He was going to have to stay under a table, or he could be a tripping hazard for the waiters and the partyers.

"Sorry pooch, I don't know what I was thinking," She said bending over to rub Sparky's head. "It's too late to take you home now, the show starts in five minutes."

"Hey Jess," called a very familiar voice, "Over here, I've saved you a seat."

"Hi, Mike, we'll be right there," She yelled across the mob of people. "Well, as soon as we can get there that is," She amended.

Weaving in and out of the crowd, Jessica shouted repeatedly, "Excuse me. I'm sorry. Coming through. Pardon me." Exasperated with the crush of people, she bent and picked Sparky up in her arms. It was much simpler than trying to steer him around their feet and watch where she was headed. "Hi Mike," She huffed as she set her twenty-five-pound pooch on the sand. "Thank you for holding a seat for me."

"My pleasure," He answered with an inviting smile. "These folks are sharing the table," he said indicating four people.

"I'm Jessica," She said, shaking hands with the man sitting beside her, "And this is Sparky," She added, "I hope you aren't allergic to dogs."

"No, no problem at all, we love dogs. It's nice to meet you, I'm Brian, and this is Lisa, Brenda, and Aaron," He motioned to the others as he said their names.

"Hi everyone," Jessica said.

"I was hoping you could come to this event, Jessica, it's apparently a crazy time." Mike said.

"It is a wild event," Brian agreed, "we were here last year, too."

"I traded shifts so that I could come," Jessica said. "I really didn't want to miss this one. It's the last big night with the celebrities. The line-up also includes the four guys that call themselves the founding-fathers. They've participated since the beginning," She indicated a group of guys noodling with their instruments. "One of their songs is really hilarious. It involves a whole lot of tequila shots, and really fast guitar picking."

Mike reached under the table and patted Sparky. "It might be a bit loud for this guy."

"I know, it was a stupid idea to bring him with me, but it's a habit. He goes most places with me," Jessica replied, twisting her bottom lip between her teeth.

"If you want, I could run him home for you," Mike offered.

The look in his eyes contradicted his words and Jessica realized he was just being kind. She shook her head, "He survived the music and noise at Carlos and Yasmin's wedding. I'm sure he'll be okay." She slipped on her sunglasses and settled into her chair at the edge of the beach, "These seats are great, and I wouldn't want to lose our spots."

She smiled to herself as she watched Mike slowly relax and meld into his chair. He seemed relieved that he didn't have fight his way out, and drive her pooch back to her house, then battle his way back through the crowd. The restaurant was jammed beyond capacity, with around three hundred people squished into the small building or onto their strip of sand. Some of the patrons stood thigh-deep in the ocean but the lucky ones had chairs. Judging by the noise level the crowd was already having a rockin' good time.

A thin brunette squeezed between customers and planted herself in front of Mike, "What would you like, handsome?" She asked in a sugary-southern accent and her smile offering more than just fetching him a drink.

Mike skimmed a self-conscious glance at Jessica. "What would you like to drink, Jess?" He asked, deliberately avoiding eye-contact with the server.

Jessica felt the woman's cold glare aimed at her, and she smiled insincerely at her before turning and responding to Mike, "A mango margarita. I haven't had one in ages."

"Good idea," He looked up at the woman, "two mango margaritas please."

The woman rolled her eyes and huffed out a breath. "Didn't you read the event information? We only have traditional margaritas, tequila shots, and beer," Her voice had lost all of the sweetness and was now bored and flat.

"Okay, that's fine, but, no salt, please."

Mike said, "make that two."

Brian held up his glass, "Bring another round for us too, please."

Without responding the woman turned and pushed through the throng, leaving Jessica and the others gaping, "What was that all about?" Asked Mike.

"I don't think Miss Personality has ever worked for tips," Jessica chuckled. She looked at Sparky who was sprawled tummy down in the damp beach sand, "What's your opinion of her, Sparky? I saw you sniffing those expensive sandals."

Sparky swished his tail and seemed to grin at Jessica, but he refrained from voicing his conclusions.

Mike laughed, "Does he ever answer you?"

"Indirectly," She said, "I can usually tell by his expressions and posture whether he likes the person, dislikes the person, or just doesn't care one way or the other."

"So, what's his verdict?"

"I think I noticed a bit of a lip-curl," She said, thoughtfully, "but his overall opinion appears to be indifference."

Mike chuckled, then added, "I'll be very surprised if we actually get drinks from Miss Personality. If she doesn't return in fifteen minutes, I'll go get them."

"No worries, I'm here for the music," *and the company too,* Jessica mentally amended.

Salt. No salt. Who gives a damn? They can just wipe it off the rim. Grabbing two margaritas with salt, Suzanne Hamilton-Forbes heard a female voice ask, "Why don't you just load up a tray and head into the crowd? It's faster, and you'll make more tips."

"Mind your own damn business," Suzanne snapped back, knowing she was incapable of balancing or carrying a tray loaded with drinks. One in each hand was her limit.

"Jeesh, I was just trying to help," the other server grumbled.

"Whatever," Suzanne headed in the general direction of the good-looking guy, the one who was sitting with the annoying blonde and her mangey mutt. The other four sitting at the same table could just damn well wait until she had a moment.

The event was turning into hard work and she hoped her idiot spouse was playing soon so that she could get this over with. She had a vial of the liquid in a small purse that she was wearing across her body. She normally wouldn't wear anything so unfashionable, but she needed a place to keep everything handy in case this suddenly went tits-up. Besides the poison, the purse contained money, her credit cards and passport, plus the keys for both the house and the golf cart.

Plunking one margarita down in front of the blonde, hard enough to cause some of the liquid to slop over the edges, she grimaced a semi-apologetic smile, then carefully set the other one in front of the man. "That's six tokens," She said.

"Thank you," replied Mike. He gave her the plastic discs, and was about to offer her a hundred-peso note as a gratuity when she abruptly pulled her hand back.

Suzanne stared with distaste at the money being offered, then turned and disappeared into the crowd. Behind her, she could hear scornful laughter.

"Hey! What about our order?" Brian shouted to her retreating back.

"Wait, did she just give you the finger?" Asked Brenda.

Jessica turned her head in time to see the woman's arm dropping down by her side. "I think she did," She laughed, then picked up her margarita and with a paper napkin wiped the salt off of the rim.

"Sorry folks, maybe yours is coming," Mike said.

"Cheers," Jessica said, as she lightly tapped her red Solo cup against Mike's, "this might be the only drink that Miss Personality brings us."

Chapter 33

February 7th Isla Mujeres

"Let's give a big, warm, island welcome to our next artist, Brandon Forbes!" Bellowed Skip Bishop, as he lifted his arms over his head and slapped his hands together with enthusiasm. The crowd responded with cheers and whistles.

Suzanne tucked her chin towards her elegant neck and pulled her hat low over her eyes as she watched the blonde-haired man perch his well-toned ass on a tall stool. Finally, her dickhead spouse, Brandon, was about start his set. His job was to crank up the crowd, to get them stomping their feet and clapping hands for the real talent. With any luck she would be far away before another performer took to the stage.

Her eyes lingered on the man that in her dewy-eyed youth she had promised to love until death. He truly was a handsome specimen, but he had promptly ignored his wedding vows and had an affair with her formerly best friend Amanda, on the one-month anniversary of their wedding day. Suzanne had stopped loving him at around infidelity number two, or maybe number three. She couldn't remember the exact day she stopped adoring him, but she sure as hell hated the weaselly rat-bastard now.

Pressing closer to the bar, Suzanne surveyed the tequila choices. Her eyes shone with cunning when she spotted Brandon's favourite, Patrón Silver. She leaned forward, catching the eye of one of the busy bartenders. "Hey, sweetie, how about a shot of Patrón for the gorgeous guy who's singing? I'll pay," She said, giving him a knowing look.

The bartender skimmed a quick glance at her and then at the musician, "Sure, it might help your chances," He leered at her.

Suzanne wanted to slap the smirk off of his face for insinuating that she wasn't pretty enough for Brandon to notice her, but she had to remain in character as a brainless server. "I surely do want me some of that sugar," She ran her tongue around her lips and winked as the bartender set the shot in front of her.

Picking up the glass, she worked her way behind the set then passed the shot of tequila to a roustabout, nodding towards the stool that held Brandon's beer. "It's a gift, but don't tell him who from just yet," She said, wishing she had worn a low-cut blouse so that the helper would focus on her tits not her face.

Unsurprised, the guy nodded absentmindedly at her. "Yeah, sure honey," He took the glass from her hand and walked on stage, then set it on an empty stool beside Brandon.

Pushing her way into the teeming mass of hot bodies, Suzanne fastened her eyes on Brandon, confirming he had noticed the glass appear beside him.

When the first song was over, he lifted the shot and gazed at the crowd, "Thank y'all whoever gave me this," and drained the glass in one swift movement. He smacked his lips, and vibrated his head like a hound shaking off water. "Damn! That was awesome!"

She smiled. *Okay.* One more shot of the expensive stuff so that he is expecting it to taste good, and then her special brew. Unsure how long he would be performing, Suzanne pushed her way back to the same bartender and said, "Hey, good-looking. Let's do that again," She pointed at the bottle of Patrón.

His tongue poked out a little, "Only if you promise me that if pretty-boy doesn't want to play, you and I can find some way to amuse ourselves."

He swayed the bottle back and forth in front of his chest while he waited for her answer.

Her skin crawling at the thought, Suzanne smiled lasciviously and said, "Sure we can, big boy."

He poured a second shot and carefully placed it in front of her, and as she reached for the glass, he placed his hand over hers. "You just remember your promise, darling. I don't like to be disappointed."

She smoothed a hand over her loose shirt, outlining her amble breasts, "You won't be disappointed." Choking back the urge to puke, she picked up the glass and turned to push her way behind the stage. The same roustabout nonchalantly took the drink from her when she pointed with her chin towards Brandon. Apparently, a woman buying shots for the good-looking musician was the norm.

She suppressed the powerful urge to snatch up the shot glass and toss the liquid in Brandon's deceitful face.

Two minutes later he reached for the glass, and held it higher, "Cheers y'all. I surely do appreciate this," He upended the drink, draining the liquid in two swallows. "Dear Lord, that is de …

lic ... i ...ous," He shivered with exaggerated pleasure.

The crowd laughed at his theatrics.

That's a good boy. Suzanne smiled to herself. *Three's the charm.*

She wormed her way back through the crowd to the same drooling bartender, "I think the shots of Patrón are improving his singing, don't you?" She simpered.

"It's improving something that's for sure," He grabbed his own crotch and gave it a squeeze, then poured the third shot and handed it to her. "Don't forget pretty lady, a promise is a promise."

Suzanne slowly ran her tongue around her lips and winked. When he had fondled his testicles, she could see his erection straining against the cloth of his shorts, then he touched the shot glass.

Low-life!

Working her way through the gyrating mass she ducked behind a screen and eyeballed the action. No one appeared to be watching her. She dumped the tequila onto the sand, then reached inside her purse and withdrew the vial of poison, uncapped it, and poured the nearly clear liquid into the glass. It didn't have the crystal clarity of the expensive tequila, but hopefully the repetition of the act would make both the stagehand and that rat-bastard Brandon complacent.

She capped the empty vial, and then edged towards the assistant. She gave him the drink and he placed it beside her soon-to-be-ex-husband.

Suzanne paused long enough to pull in a couple of breaths then slowly pushed her way out towards the street. She was torn between the hunger to watch Brandon die in agony and the overwhelming desire to escape. She heard his voice shout *cheers y'all,* and then there was pause as he consumed the liquid.

Poised at the edge of the entrance she fluffed her hair, and peered at her reflection in a store window.

Waiting. Listening. Hoping.

Then, she heard a meaty thump like a body hitting the stage and a few seconds later someone shouted, "Call an ambulance!"

Her lips jerked in approval and she stepped out on the street, walking swiftly to where she had parked the golf cart.

Chapter 34

February 7th Isla Mujeres

"Brandon!" The helper shouted as he knelt on the stage and gripped the singer's shoulder, "hey man, are you okay?"

Forbes clutched his chest, "no," he exhaled, and stilled.

"Call an ambulance!"

Jessica jumped to her feet, giving Sparky's lead to Mike, "Hold Sparky, I know some first aid, I'll see if I can do anything." She tapped shoulders, and gripped elbows, anything to get people's attention, "Please! Excuse me, let me through, I know CPR." Just as she knelt beside Brandon Forbes, she was aware of Mike arriving with Sparky in his arms.

"I was a volunteer firefighter for a few years, I can help," Mike said. He quickly set Sparky down, and looped his leash over the leg of a nearby stool, then Jessica and he rolled the man named Brandon onto his back. Mike laid two fingers on the man's carotid artery, "I don't feel a pulse and he's not breathing."

Jessica pulled off her sunglasses, and tucked them into the vee of her shirt. She said, "You start chest compressions. I'll do the rescue breathing." They worked in tandem, trying desperately to revive the man until a Red Cross attendant tapped Jessica on the shoulder. "We'll take over. And the doctora is on her way."

Jessica exhaled with relief, and shifted her body slightly letting the man acquire the rhythm before standing up and moving aside. The other attendant replaced Mike, and continued with the chest compressions.

She rubbed her lips. *Odd.* They tingled, as if the circulation was impaired. Perhaps the sensation was caused by keeping a seal on the singer's mouth while she did the rescue breathing.

Sunglasses. Her palm touched her chest, feeling for her sunglasses. She still had them. Glancing down she noticed that the tiny blue recording light was still blinking. When Brandon Forbes had started to sing, she had pushed the small button on the right temple of her sunglasses to activate the videoing feature. It had been an impulsive act, more out of curiosity than a desire to have an audio memory of the singer. Now, she pressed the small button on right temple arm and stopped the recording.

"Jessica," Mike called. He had moved further into the restaurant, and was standing with two of the municipal police.

"Yes?"

Mike pointed at a police officer standing beside him, "Sergeant Ramirez would like to speak to you."

Jessica lifted her hand, "Hey, Felipe. I'll be right there," she said, surveying the crowd. It was thinning out but still difficult to navigate with Sparky at her feet. She bent over and said, "Hugs," and he obliged by bunny-hopping into her arms. "Uff! You really are heavy. Either I need to go to the gym more often, or you need to go on a diet."

She worked her way over to Mike and the two police officers, then set Sparky down in a clear spot. "Hola Alexis. Hola Felipe."

Alexis half-smiled, but Felipe kept a neutral expression on his face. He stood with his feet squared to his shoulders, and his thumbs hooked in his utility belt. When he spoke, he sounded disturbingly similar to Comandante de Policía de Isla Mujeres, Julian Camara, who considered Jessica a meddling menace.

"So, we meet again, señorita Sanderson, over another dead body," Felipe said weightily.

"He might be okay," Jessica protested, "we just don't know yet." She glanced at Mike for support, but his troubled gaze was concentrated on the activity behind her. She turned, watching as the doctora covered the man with a sheet, "Ah crap."

Sergeant Ramirez held up his palm with his fingers spread wide, "That's the fifth."

"Fifth what?" Asked Mike.

"Body," answered Felipe, his eyes sweeping to Jessica's face, "that we've had to question señorita Sanderson about.

"Really?" Mike lobbed a startled look at Jessica.

"And that's not counting the other casualties that were linked to our murder investigations," Ramirez smiled wolfishly at Mike. "If I were you, I would be very, very careful around señorita Sanderson."

"You know damn well I'm not responsible for any of those deaths, Felipe," Jessica spat.

The sergeant grinned and wagged a finger at her, "I'm just warning señor Lyons that you are a very dangerous person to be near."

Jessica's scowl skidded away from Felipe's mocking grin and settled on Alexis.

Alexis shrugged and lightly shook her head. *Ignore him.*

"Alright, what happened here?" Felipe said, organizing his phone for note-taking.

Mike motioned to Jessica, "Ladies first."

Jessica sucked in a breath, and thought for a minute. "I wasn't focused only on Brandon Forbes. Sometimes, I watched the antics of the patrons."

"Antics?" Queried Felipe.

"The customers clowning around with friends, laughing, drinking. Bar stuff," She bounced one shoulder towards her earlobe. "It's a habit from working in the *Loco Lobo*. I look for potential troublemakers."

"So, you didn't see señor Forbes fall from his stool?"

"Not really. I wasn't focused solely on him. I did hear him hit the stage, and saw the stagehand run to his assistance."

Felipe turned to Mike Lyons, "And you señor Lyons? What did you see?"

"I didn't see him fall either. But earlier, I noticed a woman handing a shot glass of clear liquid to the stagehand, then he put the glass beside Brandon."

"I'd forgotten that," Jessica added.

"Description?" Felipe asked.

"She was our waitress, the one we named Miss Personality," Mike said to Jessica.

Felipe pinned Jessica with his dark eyes, "Miss Personality?"

"I was being sarcastic. She had zero personality for waiting on tables," Jessica replied. "She was delivering what looked like a shot of tequila, a gift from someone in the crowd. It's a pretty common occurrence at these events."

"Describe her," Ramirez demanded again.

Trying to visualize the woman, Jessica aimed her eyes at the sandy floor inside the bar, "Thin, a little taller than me. Short dark hair covered by a large floppy hat. Big sunglasses. She was wearing shorts and a baggy top," She glanced up at Felipe, "And expensive sandals."

Perplexed, Ramirez shot Jessica a glance, "What's the significance of expensive sandals?" He asked.

"Nothing really, but I know shoes. It just struck me as odd for someone who was dressed in cheap brands to be wearing pricey footwear."

Jessica rubbed her thumb and forefinger together, in a gesture meaning mucho dinero, a lot of money, "Very expensive footwear."

"I don't see the relevance of the cost of the shoes, but I've noted your observation," He said.

"Sergeant Ramirez?" A female voice said. A little procession that included the two Red Cross ambulance attendants wheeling a covered stretcher, with the Doctora walking behind, was headed to the street to load the remains of Brandon Forbes into an ambulance.

"Si, Doctora Marion, how may I help you?"

She held up a small plastic bag containing a shot glass. "This needs to be tested. Shall I arrange it? Or will you?"

Felipe Ramirez put his hand out, "Gracias. I'll take custody of that." Holding the plastic bag at eye-level, he asked, "What do you suspect?"

"I'm not sure, but it wouldn't hurt to have the contents tested," She replied, "for elimination as the cause of death."

"When will you be doing the autopsy?"

"As soon as possible. I'll call you with my results."

"Gracias, Doctora."

"De nada, Sargento." Doctora Marion turned to nod pleasantly at Mike, then shifted her gaze to Jessica. "Hello Jessica, I was told you and Mr. Lyons tried to revive Mr. Forbes."

"Yes, we tried," Jessica's smiled wanly at the doctora, "unsuccessfully it seems."

"Thank you for trying. Are you okay?"

"Yes, I'm fine."

"And you Mr. Lyons?"

"Yes, thank you Doctora. I'm okay."

"Alright, I must go, but please let me know if you have any difficulties sleeping." She settled her trade-mark straw hat on her head and briskly walked out to the street.

Jessica said to the doctora's retreating back, "She's amazing."

Chapter 35

February 7th Cancun

Detective Marco Cervera reached into his jacket pocket and extracted his buzzing phone, "Bueno," He answered, using the local greeting that encapsulated good day and hello in one word.

"Hola Detective Cervera, this is Sergeant Ramirez from the Isla Mujeres policía."

Cervera leaned back in his chair, and put his feet up on his desk. It could be a lengthy conversation and he might as well be comfortable. "Who's dead? And were Jessica Sanderson and her mutt there?"

Ironic laughter sounded in his ear, "You correctly guessed the reason for my call," Ramirez said. "We have a dead musician from Nashville, and yes, señorita Sanderson and Sparky were at the scene."

"It figures," Cervera quipped. He swung his big feet off the desk and sat up, "Nashville? Who?"

"No one you would recognize, a minor celebratory by the name of Brandon Forbes."

"You're right. I don't know that name," Cervera grunted. "How did he die?"

"We're not sure. It appears he had a heart attack. I wanted to give you and Toledo a heads-up, just in case."

"Just in case señorita Sanderson is involved in another murder," Cervera chuckled, then checked the time on his phone, "We could be there in an hour."

"No need. We've photographed everything and released the scene back to the restaurant owners," Ramirez said. "As soon as we get the autopsy results, I'll let you know."

"Claro," Cervera acknowledged.

Chapter 36

February 7th Isla Mujeres

Suzanne steered the vehicle into the driveway of the rental house and parked it. She shut off the motor and stepped out, not bothering to shut the gates or apply the security lock to the steering wheel. She planned to be here only long enough to pack her bags and arrange for the yacht service to take her back Cancun. As soon as she had that booked, she would organize a departure for herself using her private jet.

She strode purposefully down the stairs to the house, "Lupe!" She hollered. "Lupe, where are you?" Silence greeted her shout. "That stupid woman, just when I actually need her, she has buggered off." She bitched, conveniently forgetting that she had actually given Lupe the night off, not wanting her underfoot when she returned to the house.

"Freaking hell, where is that damn number?" Suzanne thumbed through the rental agreement, searching for the contact number for the yacht service. She had to get off the island as soon as possible, but didn't want to use the Ultramar passenger ferries, they were much too public. The fewer people that saw her now, the better.

Finding a general number for the company, Suzanne keyed it in to her phone and listened as it rang. After eight rings her call was picked up by an answering machine. "This is Sophia Hayden-Smith. I am renting a house on Isla Mujeres. I have a family emergency and must return to the USA as soon as possible. Call me!" She shouted her phone number into the device, then crossly punched the end-call icon.

Agitated at not connecting with a real person who could confirm that the yacht would be dispatched immediately to get her, Suzanne paced angrily back and forth across the pool deck. "Damn it all to hell," She shouted in the empty house. "Stupid backward country. I can't rely on anyone but myself." She stomped towards the bedroom, and wheeled her suitcases over to the bed. She lifted the cases onto the bed and unzipped them, then reached into the closet and yanked garments off the hangers, and tossed the clothes into the luggage. There wasn't any staff available to nicely fold and fit the items into the suitcases, and she continued to grab and toss until everything was packed.

In the next thirty minutes she left three more angry messages on the unresponsive answering machine.

"Where the hell is that piece of paper? The one with Lupe's cell number?" Then she remembered that the woman had been all smiley and sweet when she arrived, offering her phone number in case Suzanne required anything additional to her original rental agreement. She checked the front of the refrigerator, and yes, thankfully the dimwit had posted her number on a sticky note. "99-81-91-19-03," Suzanne repeated aloud as she punched in the digits.

"*Bueno*?" a female voice answered.

"Is this Lupe?" Demanded Suzanne.

"Si, señora, this is she." Luz answered with a small puff of air. *My name is Luz not Lupe.*

Suzanne could hear the woman give a little sigh. She was probably annoyed at being disturbed at home. *Well too damn bad.* This is an emergency. "I need the boat to pick me up as soon as possible tonight."

"Tonight señora?"

"Are you deaf? Yes, tonight. Book it and call me back." She hung up.

Fifteen minutes later her cell phone buzzed with an incoming call. "Yes," She barked.

"Señora Hayden-Smith?" The woman asked.

"Of course. Who did you think it would be?"

"I'm sorry, señora, the captain is not available this evening. The earliest they can send the boat will be at seven tomorrow morning."

"You call them back and remind them that I am paying a lot of money for this rental and I expect service! Do it, now!" She disconnected, resisting the urge to smash the phone on the patio. "Calm down Suzanne," She spoke aloud to the empty house. "You're making a scene, and that isn't a good plan."

Another fifteen minutes passed and again her cell phone buzzed with an incoming call, "Well?"

"Señora, I am so very sorry, but the owner of the company says that he can not so quickly accommodate your change of plans. The best that they can do is tomorrow morning at seven."

"Fine, but I am warning you, they had better be on time." She disconnected.

Chapter 37

February 7th Isla Mujeres

Curious about the latest incident involving Jessica and a dead guy, her friends had gathered inside her small home. This was body number five as Sergeant Ramirez had so helpfully pointed out earlier in the evening.

Diego Avalos was ensconced in his habitual spot, leaning against her kitchen counter just a few steps from the refrigerator and a ready supply of cold *cervesa*. Cristina had begged off, saying she should stay home with their four youngsters but to please give her love to Jessica.

Carlos and Yasmin were seated on the two kitchen chairs that they had pulled closer, into the living area. The flow of customers at the *Loco Lobo* had slowed once the *Big Daddy's* concert had started, so when Jessica called to say that she was once again tangentially involved with a death, they had left the restaurant in the hands of Isabela and had driven straight to Jessica's house.

Mike's fingers brushed Jessica's hand as he passed her a glass of wine, "Are you sure you are okay, Jess?" He asked, his eyes searching her face.

"Yep," She nodded, "I've seen bodies before, as Sergeant Ramirez was so quick to point out," She sighed deeply, and sipped the wine. She lifted her legs and balanced them on the opposite arm of the diminutive loveseat in her cozy dining-living area, then rested her head against a pillow. "Thanks for the vino, Mike."

"My pleasure," He held up the glass in a silent toast, then took a sip. "I've seen a few too, but I don't think it gets any easier," He said.

Sparky hopped onto the sofa and squeezed against her ribs, "You have enough room there, little man?" She asked Sparky, then continued speaking to Mike, "No, it doesn't get any easier." Her hand brushed the sunglasses that were still hooked in the vee of her shirt. "Huh. I wonder ..."

"What?" Yasmin asked.

She didn't answer Yasmin, instead she twisted her head towards the kitchen, "Hey, Diego, you remember these sunglasses? The ones you gave me for Christmas?" She said, holding them up so that he could see.

"Si, I do. Bought them on-line in China for ten dollars," Diego replied with a cheeky grin. "Nothing's too good for mi hermana."

Jessica grunted, "Well, just for fun I turned on the recording feature at the concert." She popped out the tiny memory chip, "I'm going to stick this in my laptop and see if anything shows up."

"Sparky, move please," She said as she gently shoved him aside and put her feet on the floor. She set her wine glass on the coffee table, and walked rapidly towards her bedroom. Two minutes later she returned with her laptop, setting it beside her glass.

"Do they actually record?" Carlos asked, pointing at the glasses.

"I've only used the feature once before and it worked, sort of," She said, clicking the mouse and downloading the video clip. Next, she opened the file, and the sound of Brandon Forbes singing came through her computer speaker. "Well, I'll be damned," She shifted so that the others could also see the screen.

"How long will it record, Jess?" Yasmin asked.

"No clue," Jessica replied. Her eyes were glued to the screen, "Although this video is amazingly good quality, considering ..." She arched an ironic eyebrow at Diego, "... the cost," she said.

"Look, there's our grouchy waitress delivering a glass of something to the helper," Mike said, pointing at the action.

"And Brandon drank it, with no obvious ill-effects," Jessica said. "Damn it, I turned my head to people watch," She said as the video swung wildly across the crowd.

"And now it's back on Brandon Forbes," Mike said as the focus swung again and returned to the musician.

This time Diego pointed at the screen, "Look, the same woman is standing behind the screen, but you can see that she just handed another shot to the stagehand."

"And again. No problem," Jessica said. "He drank it, did that fake shiver thing, and continued playing the next song. I remember him doing that."

"Here she comes again," Mike said, "I didn't realize that she delivered so many free drinks. The guy must be very popular with the ladies."

"That's pretty common in bars." Keeping her focus on the small screen Jessica said, "Looks like she handed the helper another glass, and again, he placed it on the stool beside Brandon."

"Yep," Mike said, "And down it goes."

"I didn't realize I had so much footage of him singing, I thought my head was swiveling around most of the time," Then Jessica grabbed Mike's forearm with one hand, her other one indicated the activity in the video. "Oh god, look at Brandon's face."

"This is awful," Yasmin interjected, "he looks like he's gasping for air!"

"And this is when it happens." Mike said, as they helplessly watched the singer clutch his chest and topple off the stool.

Powerless to change the inevitable outcome, Jessica dug her fingers into Sparky's curly fur, seeking comfort and reassurance. The next segment was of the crowd as Jessica apologized and elbowed her way towards the fallen man, then the recording turned sideways and the action became a jerky view of the man's arm and chest, "This is where I tucked my glasses in my shirt and helped you with CPR. The lens is slanted sideways and pointing down," She said.

Mike's calm voice could be heard over the background hubbub as he counted out the rhythm for the chest compressions; *one-one-thousand, two-one-thousand, three-one thousand.*

"You should give it to Sargent Ramirez, immediately," Carlos stated.

"Si, this video could be very helpful to the policía," Yasmin agreed.

"Madre de Dios," Diego murmured, "I had no idea those sunglasses would actually record. I only bought them as a silly Christmas gift."

Jessica grabbed her cell phone, and scrolled through her contacts to find Felipe's number. She pointed at the computer with her free hand, "that's where I figured out the video might still be running, and I turned it off." The video wobbled as Jessica lifted the glasses from her shirt and shut off the recording function.

Sparky could be seen sniffing the area around the stool that he was loosely tied to, then the screen went black.

Chapter 38

February 7th Isla Mujeres

"Bueno," Ramirez' voice sounded in her ear.

"Felipe, this is Jessica. I have something important to show you." Jessica said, foregoing the expected greeting and polite questions on his and his family's health. "You need to come to my house, immediately."

"Tranquilo," Ramirez replied. "What's going on, Jessica?"

"I've a video of Brandon Forbes when he was performing today."

"Okay?"

"It shows him drinking something, then clutching his chest and falling off the stool."

"Okay. Don't play it again until we get there," Ramirez said. Jessica could hear him shout Alexis' name just before he ended the call.

Jessica unlocked the front door, and left it slightly ajar to give Felipe and Alexis easy access. She paced impatiently inside her small house. "This is awful, Mike. We were right there and couldn't prevent his murder."

"We don't know for certain that's what happened, Jess," Mike said, "The doctora has to do an autopsy first."

"I know, but it sure looks like he was deliberately poisoned," She pulled her long blonde plait forward, over one shoulder and fiddled with the end of the braid.

A siren wailed in the distance, increasing in volume as it neared her home, "Felipe," Diego snorted, "He loves the adrenaline rush of speeding to a scene, even when it isn't a life and death emergency."

Jessica walked to her front door, and opened it fully, "And my neighbours are poking their noses outside to see what happening - again - at the crazy gringa's house."

"You do lead an exciting life," Diego said, with a teasing grin.

"Not my fault!" She retorted.

The squad car skidded to a stop, blocking the street. Sergeant Ramirez and Constable Gomez scrambled out, leaving the roof-rack strobing with an eye-stabbing combination of red, blue, and white lights. "Show us the video please," Ramirez demanded, barely slowing down he strode into Jessica's house.

Jessica hit play, and stood aside to let Felipe and Alexis have a better view. "This is where she delivers the drinks," Jessica indicated the glass being handed to the helper; once, twice, and a third time. "He drank the third glass, then clutched his chest and fell over," She added, "And that's where I was trying to get through the crowd. Now Mike and I are doing CPR, and then I shut off the recording."

"Do you want to see it again?" Asked Mike.

"No, but I need to take that flash drive with me as evidence," He pulled a small plastic bag out of his jacket pocket, and opened it, "please put the memory card in here."

"My fingerprints are on it," Jessica responded. "Is that going to be a problem for me?" She pinched the edge of the card between her thumb and forefinger, uneasily contemplating the evidence bag that Felipe held out to her. In her opinion, the Mexican justice system was not as open or as fair as the Canadian system. Any dealings with the policía, even Felipe and Alexis, made her edgy with uncertainty.

"No, don't worry." Felipe said, "I'll explain the situation."

She pulled her hand back, "You do realize that Comandante Camara hates me, right?"

"Hates you? No," Felipe shook his head, "Thinks you are an infuriating nuisance that should be immediately deported back to Canada? Absolutely." He impatiently shook the bag, "Just give me the damn jump drive, Jessica."

She reluctantly dropped the tiny device into the bag, and reached into her pocket to pull out a handful of Mexican peso bank notes, then handed the money to Mike.

Holding the money in his open palm Mike quietly watched her with a befuddled expression while she explained, "This will help cover my expenses while I am incarcerated," She said. "Please arrange for someone to bring me food and water at the jail, at least twice a day. Meals aren't provided for prisoners. And please make sure one of my friends looks after Sparky until I can negotiate payment for my release."

"Stop poking the bear, Jessica," Felipe growled, "You're your own worst enemy when it comes to the Comandante."

"Whatever," She retorted. She gave Mike a wry smile as she reclaimed her cash and stuffed it back in the pocket of her shorts. "The man is a corrupt buffoon."

Felipe shook his head, "Let it go, Jessica." He motioned to Alexis that they were leaving.

Carlos held up his hand, "Felipe, wait a minute, por favor."

Felipe stopped and looked at him, obviously waiting for an explanation.

Jessica glanced sideways at Carlos, "What's up? You've been really quiet since I played this video."

He pulled out his phone, "Just give me a moment to check something," He said, punching in a number. "Hola Luz, this is Carlos. Do you have a minute?"

"Si, jefe, how can I help?" She replied.

"I'm with Jessica, and few others, including Sergeant Ramirez and Constable Gomez. Do you mind if I put you on speaker?" Carlos asked.

"No, it's fine," She answered uncertainly.

He pushed the button, "Can you hear me Luz?"

"Si."

"Luz, can you describe the woman who is renting the big house at Punta Sur?"

225

"Señora Sophia?"

"Is that her name?"

"Si, Sophia Hayden-Smith," Luz said.

"What does she look like?" Asked Carlos. He noticed Alexis typing notes using an app on her phone.

"Tall, thin, short dark hair with blonde highlights, and brown eyes," Luz said.

Jessica nodded and whispered, "That sounds like our waitress."

Keeping eye contact with Felipe, Carlos continued to ask questions of Luz, "Do you know if she went out this afternoon?"

"I don't know, jefe. She told me to take half of the day off, so I left at two today."

Carlos' eyebrows shot up into his hairline, "Half a day off? But I thought she was a demanding guest."

"She has been, but today she was all smiles when she told me to leave early," Luz explained. "Why do you want to know about the señora?"

"I'm just curious," He temporized, "One more question. What does she normally wear?"

Carlos ignored Felipe's scornful look. "Why is that important?" The cop whispered.

"She has only been on the island for three days, and I have only ever seen her in shorts, and a loose blouse."

"What about her footwear?" Carlos probed.

"Oh, yes, she likes really expensive shoes."

Jessica snapped her fingers, and pointed at Felipe, "It's her, our waitress," She quietly said.

"Maybe," Felipe rumbled, "Or maybe not."

"Anything else that you can think of Luz?" Asked Carlos.

"No jefe, but if you told me why you are asking, I might be able to think of something more helpful."

"I can't really explain right now, Luz, but you have been very helpful. Please give my best to Rodrigo."

"Sure, okay, Carlos. I will. Adios."

Carlos ended the call and said, "Watching that video reminded me of something that Luz had told her husband Rodrigo, who told me." Carlos explained, "The woman likes expensive shoes," He pointed at the jump drive stashed in the evidence bag, "And even I can see that the shoes she was wearing at the concert didn't match the cheap outfit she had on."

"Told ya," Jessica said.

Felipe rolled his eyes, and blew air out of his mouth.

"I didn't know you were such a fashionista, Carlos," Alexis ribbed him.

Carlos grinned and pointed at Yasmin, "My beautiful wife is a fashionista. I always listen carefully to what she tells me."

"Right," Yasmin said with a touch of sarcasm.

Carlos' cell phone vibrated in his hand with another call from Luz, "Hang on Felipe, one more minute," He said.

"Hola Carlos, with all the questions you were asking I forgot to tell you," Luz said, "the señora wanted to book the boat back to Cancun this evening."

"Tonight? She wanted to leave tonight?" Carlos queried. "Did she say why?"

Yes, tonight," Luz confirmed, "but the boat won't be available until tomorrow morning, at seven. She said she had an emergency back in the Estados Unidos."

"That's interesting, very interesting. Thank you, Luz." He disconnected the call, and looked at the others, "It appears that the woman renting the

Twisted Isla

big house in Punta Sur wants to leave our little
island paradise as soon as possible. I wonder why
that is?"

Chapter 39

February 7th Isla Mujeres

"Shouldn't we bring her in for questioning?" Alexis said to Felipe Ramirez.

"No, not yet. La señora isn't going anywhere until tomorrow morning."

"But what if she decides to leave on one of the passenger ferries?" Alexis asked, keeping the tone of her voice light. She didn't understand why Felipe wanted to wait until the morning to interrogate the woman, but she had to tread lightly. He was wearing his stubborn look; the one that said, why are you questioning me. He could become sullen and difficult if she publicly doubted his decisions. It was the disadvantage of being both lovers and co-workers, and him having the higher rank.

Felipe stared quietly at her before answering, "I'll arrange for a constable to watch the house. La señora won't be able to leave without me knowing about it," He stated. "If she tries to leave, then we'll pick her up."

He motioned towards the door, "Let's go, Constable Gomez."

Alexis started towards the door, but Felipe was still blocking the exit. He turned to Jessica and said, "I want you and Mike to come with us tomorrow morning, to identify the woman."

"In the police cruiser?" Jessica asked.

"No, you can drive in your own vehicle. I just want you to look at the woman, and tell me if she is the same person who was your waitress at the concert."

"Ah, o-kay," Jessica agreed, "but couldn't we identify her anonymously somehow?" She shot Alexis a questioning glance.

Alexis remained silent with her eyes locked on Jessica's. She moved her head in a slight negative signal.

"We don't have an interrogation room with fancy one-way mirrors," Felipe snapped at her. "Don't worry, nothing bad will happen to you."

Jessica snuck a look at Mike. He mouthed, *oh well*, and gave her a reassuring smile. "Okay, we'll meet you there. What time?"

"Meet us at the gate at six-thirty. The boat is scheduled to pick her up at seven," He said turning to leave.

"Six-thirty Mexican time?" Jessica asked, unable to resist the chance to goad Felipe. Tardiness was a common Mexican trait; they habitually didn't arrive on time for anything including life-changing events like weddings or funerals. Appointments were fluid and a two-hour delay wasn't unusual. But in this case, if they weren't on time a suspected murderer would escape and then Felipe would have to ask the State Police to detain her before she got to the airport. The two State detectives, that she had nicknamed Frick and Frack, would have a great laugh at the expense of Ramirez.

Felipe turned back, leveled his dark eyes at Jessica, and said, "No, señorita Sanderson, six-thirty. Sharp."

"Yes sir," She answered, then pressed her lips tightly together. Sometimes Felipe didn't appreciate her humour.

As the door shut firmly behind the departing policía, Mike said to Jessica, "You just can't resist tweaking him, can you?"

Jessica placed her palm flat on her breastbone, "Me?" She protested.

"You left a message for me?" The voice asked.

"Si. Do you know who this is?" Asked Bruno Torres. The voice on the cell phone belonged to the Cancun captain Damien Hau, whom Torres had used in the past for transporting drugs to the island.

"Of course."

"I need a ride off the island," Torres said. The policía had impounded his truck and were most likely searching for him, so he was forced to change his plans. He had wanted to work the usual half-day on Saturday, collect his week's wages, and drive the truck off the island. Then after a brief stop at the apartment to collect his stash he intended to head towards the anonymity of Mexico City; just one more insignificant person in a megalopolis of twenty-eight million souls.

"When?"

"Immediately."

"I can't do it immediately," Hau answered. "The earliest I can help you is early tomorrow morning. I'm scheduled to pick up a single passenger from a house near Punta Sur," He said.

233

"I've room for a cash customer," indicating that he intended to keep the money for himself.

"How much?" Bruno asked, knowing he would probably agree to the price no matter what the other man said, but he didn't want to appear to be too eager. He couldn't use the passenger ferries because the policía would be watching for him, and the terminal had security cameras everywhere.

Hau quoted an amount that was, under the circumstances, quite reasonable.

"Okay," Bruno agreed, "But won't your client ask questions?"

"I'll deal with that. There is a full-time maid at the house. I'll tell her you are a new guy from the island who has just started working with us, that way she won't ask awkward questions."

"Where do I meet you?"

Hau described the house, and where it was located.

"I know the house you mean," Torres stated. "What time?"

"Be on the dock no later than six-thirty," Hau said, then added, "And one more thing, wear navy pants or shorts, and a plain white shirt. You're an employee, remember."

"Claro. See you tomorrow." Torres ended the call, and stuffed the phone in his pocket. *Where the hell could he find navy pants at this time of night? Maybe at Chedraui. They're open until ten.*

An hour later Torres left Chedraui, the local version of a super-store, with two items clutched in his hand; navy pants, and a white shirt. *Bonus.* He tucked his parcel in the storage compartment under the seat, then pressed the starter on his Yamaha, and powered away.

Tonight, he was forced to crash at a cheap hotel in Centro. Tomorrow he would escape on Hau's boat and then disappear, but he was uncertain about stopping at the apartment.

To start a new life, he needed the cash he had taken from Chab's safe, but Gaby wasn't answering his phone calls.

She wouldn't have the nerve to report him to the cops...would she?

Chapter 40

February 8th Isla Mujeres

"You, take those to the dock," the woman barked and pointed at her two large bags sitting just inside her bedroom door. Angling her head to briefly check her image in the mirror she pressed her lips together to smooth out her lipstick, then she glided out of the room.

Bruno Torres briefly caught a sympathetic glance from the maid, Luz, before he shifted his seething glare away. He roughly snapped the handles of the suitcases into the extended position, and stalked out of the house heading towards the dock.

Glancing towards the ocean Torres recognized the sound and the shape of Hau's cruiser slowing as it neared the shoreline. He could hear Hau throttling back the twin engines as he lined up to the wharf in preparation for docking.

Torres thumped his way down the stone stairway, roughly dragging the luggage.

"Be careful you clumsy idiot!" The woman yelled at his retreating back.

Torres imagined grabbing her from behind and silently slicing her skinny throat. He could almost feel the hot gush of blood and the weight of her lifeless body as she slumped backwards against his chest. Fortunately for her, he was in a hurry to leave the island and killing her would complicate his plans.

The captain, Damien Hau, leapt lightly onto the wharf, and secured the bowline, then walked to the stern with one hand on the safety rail, to keep the cruiser in position while he secured the second line.

Torres admired the man's easy proficiency with boats. He rarely needed the assistance of a deck hand for docking. Torres held up a hand in greeting, but didn't say anything. He would take his cues from Hau.

"Hi, you must be my new deckhand," Hau said, extending his right hand to shake with Torres.

"Si, I am." Torres replied, giving Hau a tight smile.

"Welcome aboard, you can stow those cases at the back," Hau pointed to the stern.

Torres nodded his head and dragged the luggage to the rear. He pulled them up the ramp and secured the bags in a storage area.

Behind him he could hear Hau speaking in a groveling tone to the obnoxious bitch. "Yes, the sea is very calm this morning señora. It will be an uneventful trip," Hau said, then spoke to Luz, "Hola Luz."

"Hola Damien," She answered, then Torres heard a cell phone ring, and the maid's voice answering. "Bueno. Si, yes, we are," And then her voice faltered.

Curious Torres glanced back at the maid. She had turned her shoulder to the group and was speaking quietly into her phone.

Luz ended the call, and shifted her gaze to the captain, "Uno momento, Damien, I must check the house one more time to ensure that the señora hasn't left anything behind."

"I'm not an imbecile," Snapped the woman, "I haven't forgotten anything."

"I'm sorry, señora, it is the policy of my employers," Luz stammered, as she rapidly retreated up the stone stairway.

Torres snapped his fingers at Hau, to draw his attention. He jutted his chin towards the retreating maid, "Vámonos?" He was asking if they should leave.

Hau looked towards the house, then back at Torres, "I'll give Luz a minute or two to check for forgotten items."

"No me gusta," Torres mumbled. His gaze swept upwards to the pathway leading up the embankment. The upper floors were easily visible, but the main level and the stairway leading from the street to the living area were hidden at this angle. "I think we should leave," He reiterated, in Spanish.

"Tranquilo," Hau said, making a calming motion with his right hand.

"Speak English!" The woman barked.

"I'm very sorry, señora, my assistant is new. He was asking about our procedures once we reach the other side," Soothed Hau. He extended his hand to guide her up the ramp and onto the boat. "Would you prefer to sit inside madam, or outside in the fresh air?"

"Inside."

"Of course, as you wish," Hau said offering her a hand.

"I'm at the house now," Luz whispered into her cell phone to her husband, "Where are you?"

"We've just arrived at the gate. Go inside and stay away from the windows," Rodrigo responded.

"Who's with you?"

"The six policía, plus Jessica, Carlos, Yasmin, and Mike Lyons is now part of the crew," He said with a hint of laughter in his voice.

"No Sparky?" Luz questioned, knowing that Jessica rarely went anywhere without him.

"On board the *Bruja del Mar* with Diego and Pedro. They wanted him as their backup."

"Backup?"

"He has sharp teeth. They want to be prepared for anything."

"Please, be careful mi amor," Luz said. "Whenever Jessica is involved there is always trouble."

Rodrigo barked a short laugh, "I know, I'm keeping away from her."

"But why are the policía looking for señora Hayden-Smith?"

"They think she poisoned that singer yesterday."

"Poisoned?" Luz felt sick at the idea.

"Yes, the doctora was able to confirm that he was poisoned," Rodrigo said.

"That's awful."

"Just a minute," Rodrigo said, then after a short pause he asked, "Sergeant Ramirez wants to know how many people are on board?"

"Only three. The captain Damian Hau, a new deckhand, and the señora."

"Okay," He replied, then she heard him say, "three on board," presumably to Ramirez.

Luz snuck up to the window and glanced down at the dock, "Rodrigo, they're casting off!"

She heard him shout, "Ramirez, they're leaving!"

Ramirez responded with, "Go. Go. Go."

Then she was listening to dead air.

"Something isn't right. We need to leave, now," Torres said to Hau, as he rapidly unwound the rear mooring line.

Hau glanced up towards the house then back at Torres. He didn't see any problems but Torres was jumpy. "Okay, cast off," he said as he started the starboard engine, and then reached for the ignition button on the portside motor.

Running to the stern of the vessel, Torres shouted. "Go now. Go. Go."

Hau skimmed a look at the house, and saw six uniformed policía charging down the stairway, headed straight for the dock. "Freaking hell, Torres, what have you got me into?" He cursed.

"Just get us out of here. I'll pay extra." Torres scrambled to untie the stern line, and tossed the rope in an untidy heap on the deck.

"What's going on?" The woman popped her head out of the cabin and shouted at Hau.

"Sit down and shut the hell up!" Bellowed Torres, he whipped out his knife, and pointed it at her, "Or, I'll shut you up. Permanently."

As the boat powered away from the dock the woman grabbed the doorway for support and snarled at Torres, "You ridiculous little man. You have no idea of who you are dealing with," Her lips curled in distaste, then she turned to Hau. "I will make it worth your while if you get me to Cancun," She said, then pointed at Torres, "and you can toss this piece of trash overboard to distract the police."

"You stupid bitch, no one is tossing me anywhere," Torres growled, waving his sharp knife closer to her throat. She glared into his eyes, and didn't flinch.

"Sit down!" Hau yelled, "Both of you, sit down and shut up!"

Torres could hear the anxiety in Hau's voice. Keeping both the woman and the captain in his line of sight, he asked, "¿Que pasa?"

"We have company," Hau pointed at the larger boat bearing down on them.

"You gotta gun?"

"I know these guys. I'm not going to shoot them."

"Can you ram them?"

"And then what? My boat will be damaged too." Hau snuck a speculative look at the woman. "Who are the policía looking for? You, señora? Or my insignificant friend?"

"I have no idea what you mean," She bit back.

Twisted Isla

"Why are you in such a hurry to get to Cancun," Hau asked, arcing his boat away from the oncoming vessel.

"I have a very important business meeting in the United States," She retorted.

Damien Hau caught Torres' eye, and bounced his chin towards the water. "Swim for it. I'll keep them occupied," He said in Spanish, while studying the woman.

"Claro," Torres quickly stripped off his shirt, pants, and deck shoes and slid over the railing as smoothly as an otter entering the water.

Hau glanced briefly to make sure Torres was clear of the propellers then powered forward towards the approaching sport fishing boat. Torres was a strong swimmer and had a good chance of escaping. The woman on the other hand, was as nasty as a viper hiding in the long grass. His Spidey-sense was telling him that she was the person that the policía wanted.

He slowed down and shouted across the water to the big man that he knew was Diego Avalos, "Hola Diego. What's up?"

Avalos cupped his hands around his mouth and shouted back, "Return to the dock, Damien. The policía would like to speak to you."

"Why?" He asked, giving Torres a bit more time to escape.

"They want to speak to your passenger."

Hau turned to the woman whom he knew as Sophia Hayden-Smith. "I don't know what your story is, but I hope you have a good lawyer."

The look on her face was one of pure malice, "Shut. Up."

Chapter 41

February 8th Isla Mujeres

"Whoa, careful little guy, these decks are slippery," Diego said grabbing for Sparky's collar. "What's all the excitement about bud?"

Pedro turned his head to see what was happening behind him, while keeping one eye on the Hau's cruiser. "What's up? Why is he barking?"

"I'm not sure. He's pretty excited. He's been running up and down the deck, searching for something in the water."

"Dolphins?"

"I don't know," Keeping one hand on Sparky's collar, Diego leaned over the railing and peered into the crystalline sea, "What are you so interested in, little buddy?" The white sand floor of the ocean enabled him to clearly see a long shape powering through the water. He laughed, "Oh-ho, I'm going to need the hook to haul this one on board."

"This what?"

Diego pointed at the water, "that," he said as a head broke the surface. A man gulped in air and dove again, powering forward with strong strokes.

Pedro eased the throttles back, and positioned the boat parallel to the swimmer. "What do you think he weighs?"

"Maybe seventy kilos, más o menos, around hundred and sixty pounds. He's looks pretty fit and might put up a good fight, but we'll get him," Diego answered, his eyes tracking the underwater form.

"Let's not work too hard at hauling him in. We'll just keep him company until he tires out," Pedro said. "Good job, Sparky."

Diego released Sparky's collar and rubbed his ears, "Si, really good job, little buddy." He did a quick check to make sure that Hau was behaving and heading back to the dock, then perched on the gunnel where he could comfortably keep an eye on the swimmer.

Sparky leaned over the edge and stared into the water as a shockingly deep growl vibrated out of his compact body.

"Easy, bud, we'll get him," Diego said, just as the man broke the surface for more air. "Give it up pendejo. We can do this all day."

The guy defiantly flipped him the finger, and dove once more to swim a few hundred meters.

"He's slowing down," Pedro said.

"It won't be long now."

The swimmer popped to the surface and inhaled loudly. Treading water he glared at Diego and heaved in a few big breaths.

"You ready for a lift yet?" Diego asked, without moving from his comfortable perch.

The man cursed and started swimming towards the stern. Pedro slipped the twin engines into neutral, and turned his seat around to keep an eye on their new arrival.

Diego leaned slightly forward, reached under his legs, and wrapped his hand around a heavy wooden bat, their fish whacker. *No sense taking chances with the guy.*

"Give me a hand," The man said as he grasped the edge of the swim-grid.

"No, just get your ass on board."

Hanging onto a metal cleat and balancing one foot on the propeller the swimmer pulled himself out of the water.

Barking loudly Sparky scrambled through the gate and landed with an ungainly thump on the swim-grid.

A strong brown hand reached out and gripped Sparky by the scruff of his neck, then flung him into the ocean and away from the boat.

The only sound Sparky made was one surprised, *yip*, followed by a splash and frantic paddling motions.

The man surged forward aiming his shoulder towards Diego's chest.

Diego raised the bat and whacked the guy on the side of the head: hard.

He crumpled to the deck, with a moan. Blood ran from a head wound.

"Pedro, keep an eye on him. I'll get Sparky." Diego shoved the bat at Pedro then dove into the water and swam robustly towards the dog.

"Come on little guy, we know you don't like deep water," He tucked one arm around Sparky and awkwardly side-stroked back to the swim grid. "We're going to be in so much trouble with your mama." He said.

Chapter 42

February 8th Isla Mujeres

Jessica and Mike stood to one side on the private dock of the rental house, waiting for Ramirez to tell them what he wanted them to do next. Suddenly she heard her normally quiet dog barking loudly. It was the deep booming sound he made when someone had been outside her house and stealing fuel from her golf cart.

Worried, she scrutinized the *Bruja del Mar*. The boat was slowly moving forward and she could see both Diego and Sparky leaning over the side.

"Mike," She said, pointing towards the *Bruja*, "what do you think is happening out there?"

He raised his eyes, taking in the scene, "It looks like they are watching something in the water. Maybe it's a turtle or dolphin."

"Yeah, maybe," She temporized, "but Sparky only barks when he sees or hears something he doesn't like."

"Shut it down!" Sergeant Ramirez yelled.

Startled by the forcefulness of his voice, Jessica's attention swung from Sparky to Ramirez.

He was glaring at Hau while striking an aggressive stance. One hand rested on his gun holster and his were feet planted shoulder-width apart on the dock while the police constables scurried to grab the railings of the craft fore and aft, holding it against the wharf. The scene reminded her of something out of a Monty Python movie.

Hau turned off the engines then calmly placed both of his hands on the steering wheel, in full view of the sergeant.

"I'm coming aboard," Ramirez stated, instead of requesting Hau's permission to board.

"I need to secure the lines," Hau said, "am I allowed do that?"

"Yes, just don't make any sudden moves. I'm armed." The introduction of armed police officers was a recent change of policy for the municipality, and from Jessica's vantage point Ramirez appeared to be reminding Hau that any funny business would be met with deadly force.

"Claro."

"Search the entire boat," Commanded Ramirez, indicating with a flick of his hand that his constables should spread out to either end.

Hau lifted a mooring line then stepped onto the dock and tied the rope to a cleat, "What are you looking for Sergeant?" He asked, "Perhaps I could help you."

"We can handle this," Ramirez snapped.

"Okay," Hau continued with his task of tying up. From Jessica's vantage point he looked as if he was completely unfazed by the police presence, and then he fumbled a mooring line, dropping it on the wharf.

"What is the meaning of this?" Demanded a shrill voice, "I have a flight to catch." A thin woman wearing a large straw hat came into view.

Standing on the dock, Jessica shot Mike an amused glance, "She certainly sounds and looks like our waitress, Miss Personality."

"Yes, she does," Mike agreed.

Ramirez shot a quick glance to where Mike and Jessica were standing; Jessica bobbed her head, *yes that's her*. She could hear Ramirez say to the woman, "We have a few questions for you señora. You'll be coming into the police station with us."

"I will not!"

"Come quietly with me señora, or I will handcuff and arrest you."

"I demand to have a lawyer present," She snapped.

"Good for you. Once we get to the station, I will call the local notario, but in the meantime you are coming with me." Ramirez replied, as he reached out to grasp her elbow.

"Take your hands off of me!" She shouted.

Jessica saw a blur of motion and heard the slap of skin against skin. "Oh, oh, bad move. Never hit a cop." She inched closer to the *Bruja del Mar* so that she had a better view of the action. She could now clearly see the woman who had been their server yesterday afternoon and she whispered to Mike, "Yep, it's definitely her. Miss Personality."

From the back deck of the boat, Ramirez said, "You are now under arrest for assaulting a police officer," then he spun the woman around and snapped on the handcuffs.

"You can't do this. It's illegal."

"Señora it is illegal to strike a police officer, in any country, please be quiet," Ramirez replied.

Listening to the exchange Jessica was quite certain that Sergeant Ramirez was happy to have an excuse to handcuff the woman. She knew he detested arrogant women, and he especially detested arrogant foreign women.

Jessica knew from past experience that the best way to handle Ramirez was to appeal to his macho vanity and keep your opinions to yourself. After a few head-to-head clashes she had finally got the hang of handling him. It could be said that they were friends now – well, more like friendly adversaries.

Chapter 43

February 8th Isla Mujeres

Pedro eased the *Bruja del Mar* up to the dock and Diego jumped off, securing the bow by double-wrapping the line around the cleat.

Sparky leapt onto the dock, and raced towards Jessica, dripping a trail of water as he ran.

"Sergeant Ramirez. We have a little gift for you," Diego shouted.

"Sparky," Jessica opened her arms and bent over. As he neared her, he stopped and vigorously oscillated his body, spraying water on her face and body. "Augh. Thanks a lot. Why are you wet?" She asked him. He skidded face down across the dock, scrubbing his chin and shoulder on the rough surface then shook his fur again; his method of drying off.

Ramirez moved onto the back deck, towing the woman by her elbow. "A gift? What do you mean, Diego?"

Diego pointed at a man wearing only wet underpants standing on the wharf beside the *Bruja del Mar*. He was holding a bloody cloth against his head. "This guy was swimming away from Hau's cruiser. We thought you might want to speak to him so we offered him a ride back."

Ramirez pointed at the man's head, "Offered?"

"He tried to knock me overboard, and his head accidentally connected with my fish bat."

"Does he need a doctora?"

"You probably should get someone to look at him," Diego conceded.

"I wonder why he is so keen to avoid us?" Ramirez said, then looked at the pair of pants and shirt that were laying on the rear deck. He lifted the pants, "these appear to be your size, amigo," he said, rifling through the pockets for identification.

Holding a slim wallet in his hands, Ramirez tossed the clothes at the nearest constable, "Take these to him and make sure he gets dressed." He flipped open the wallet and removed the driver's license. His eyes quickly scanned the information and he barred his teeth in a predatory grin.

"Señor Torres, it's a pleasure to finally meet you. Our esteemed compañeros of the Cancun

256

State Police have been looking for you," Ramirez said.

"I need my shoes," Torres replied.

Ramirez picked up the sneakers and threw them on the wharf, then pointed at the constable, "As soon as he's dressed, handcuff him and put him in the truck. I'll ask the doctora to come to the station to check his injury."

Ramirez turned to Hau, "You too Damien. I have questions for you."

"Come on, Ramirez. I don't know anything about this guy. He's a new-hire for our company. Today was his first day," Hau grumbled.

"So, if I call your head office, they'll back up your story?" Ramirez pinned Hau with a steely glare.

Jessica was closely watching the interaction between the two men, and she saw the look of defeat flicker across Hau's face.

"Fine," he said, removing the keys from the ignition and securing the door to the inside salon.

"I think Damien is involved in something shady," She whispered as an aside to Mike.

"You know him?" Asked Mike.

"I don't actually know him, but I know who he is. It's a small island. Everyone knows everyone," She said, turning to Diego. "But the real question is why is Sparky wet?"

"Um. He went for a little swim," Diego answered without looking at her.

"A swim? He's terrified of deep water."

Diego guiltily lifted his eyes and met hers, "He was a little overexcited when Torres pulled himself onto the swim-grid. Sparky got too close, and Torres tossed him into the water."

"Oh my God, was he hurt?"

"I don't think so. He only yipped once. I dove in and gave him a lift back to the boat."

"Damn it, Diego …"

"Listen up everyone," Ramirez shouted, interrupting Jessica's lecture, "report to the police station. And that includes you," He said, looking directly at Jessica.

She refrained from answering with a caustic remark. She just wanted this over and done. Looking at Mike, she pointed at the stairway, "Shall we?"

"Sure."

"Come on Sparky," She patted her leg, signalling him to stay close. "I have another leash and harness in the golf cart," She added as an aside to Mike.

Nearing the top of the climb, Sparky suddenly veered to the left and dashed into the garden. "Sparky! Come here," She said, with a hint of asperity.

"I'll get him, Jess," Mike said.

Annoyed at Sparky for disappearing, Jessica huffed out a breath and followed Mike. She found the two of them inspecting a smelly pile of decomposing vegetation. "What's so interesting?"

"I have no idea," Mike said, bending over and picking up Sparky. "Let's go little man, we have an appointment at the police station."

Chapter 44

February 8th Isla Mujeres

"All of the usual troublemakers including the wonder-mutt, Sparky," Detective Cervera said, surveying the crowded room in the Isla Mujeres Municipal Police station. His scrutiny settled on Mike Lyons, "And do we have a new addition to Sparky's entourage?"

"Detective Frick, this is my friend Michael Lyons from Canada," Jessica dead-panned. "Michael, these two gentlemen are Detective Cervera, otherwise known as Frick, and his partner Detective Toledo, or Frack."

Cervera sighed, rocked up on his toes, and jammed his fingers into his front pockets. He gave Jessica a shrewd look, "You know, I can have you deported for your disrespect to the policía."

"So, you keep telling me," She acknowledged, "And yet, here I am, still driving you loco."

Cervera shot a long-suffering look at Ramirez, "Can't you control her?"

"No," Ramirez shook his head, "She treats me with an equal amount of insolence."

"All right, run me through this, before I chat with your prisoner," Cervera said.

"Actually, I'm sure you will be interested in both of my prisoners," Ramirez replied with a tight smile.

"Why?"

"Remember you asked us to check for a black crew-cab with the placa ending in 476?"

"Si."

Ramirez pointed in the direction of the holding cells, "We found it and the owner. The truck belongs to one Bruno Torres, currently relaxing in one of our luxurious guest-suites," He said, meaning the bare concrete cell barely large enough to hold a set of narrow bunk beds and a seatless toilet.

"When did you arrest him?"

"Early this morning. He was on the same boat, or perhaps I should say *in* the same boat, as the señora. We wanted to question her in connection with the death of Brandon Forbes," Ramirez answered.

261

"Both were on the same boat? Headed to Cancun?"

"Si."

"How did you know he would be there?"

Ramirez grinned, displaying bright white teeth accented by his dark skin, "We didn't, and he seemed very reluctant to talk to us. He slipped over the side and tried to swim away. Sparky spotted him first, then Pedro and Diego convinced him to get into their boat." He said, nodding in the direction of the two men.

"Gracias," Cervera said, nodding at them, "Now, bring me up to date on the suspected murder of señor Forbes.

"We'll start with this video that Jessica recorded at the concert," He said tapping the play button on his laptop. "Watch the woman in the background handing drinks to the stagehand. The video is quite long, so I'll skip ahead when necessary." He said, tapping the play icon.

The group watched in glum silence as the video re-played again the inevitable sequence of events.

"Madre de Dios," Toledo murmured when Forbes clutched his chest and toppled off the stool.

"There's more," Ramirez said, "this is where Jessica and señor Lyons were trying to revive señor Forbes," He pointed at the screen. "And this is where she turned off the camera function of her sunglasses."

"A camera in your sunglasses?" Cervera shot Jessica an incredulous look. "May I?" He held out his hand, indicating that he wasn't asking for permission.

"Si," She handed them to Cervera, "The record button is on the right side. A small blue light will flash when the recording feature is activated."

He pushed the button, "I don't see a blue light."

"That's because the memory chip is in the computer, not the sunglasses," motioning to the laptop Jessica's lips twitched with the beginning of a smirk.

Cervera cocked his index finger, "Don't."

She clamped her mouth shut but the insolence sparkled in her eyes.

"I mean it. Don't do it."

"Of course, Detective Cervera."

"Detective," Carlos said.

Cervera smoothed his irritated expression and faced Carlos, "¿Si, señor Mendoza?"

"Luz Hernandez, my good friend, and former housekeeper told me a few interesting things about the woman who was arrested this morning." Carlos said.

"What things?"

"Luz thinks the woman was boiling something in the kitchen."

Cervera raised one shoulder indicating a lack of interest, "Cooking is not a crime, unless she is a terrible cook."

"Luz mentioned the woman seemed to be boiling something like a plant or branches. She used one of the very large pots but didn't clean it properly and Luz could feel a scummy residue on the inside of the pot. Luz said the residue caused a tingling sensation in her fingertip when she touched it," Carlos said, "And the woman seemed very interested in the garden plants, carefully checking each one as if she was searching for a particular type."

Jessica snapped her fingers, "Mike, remember when we were walking back up the stairway, and Sparky veered off to smell that pile of garden refuse?"

"Yeah, I do."

She turned to Cervera, "My pooch was really interested in a mushy pile of leaves and branches that had been tossed from the upper deck into the flower garden. I wonder if that was what she had been boiling?"

Cervera studied her for a few moments, then turned to Ramirez. "Can you send someone to get a sample?"

Ramirez motioned with his finger, "Jess, you and Sparky, come with me. Show me the stuff that wonder-mutt was interested in."

"Wait, I just remembered something else," Jessica said.

"What?"

"My lips tingled after we tried to resuscitate Brandon Forbes." She rubbed her lips again, remembering the odd sensation. "I wonder if I was exposed to the poison?"

Back at the rental house Jessica hopped out of the police cruiser and tugged lightly on Sparky's leash. "Come on pup, let's have a look at that smelly gunk."

Ramirez carelessly slammed his driver's door causing the car to rock a little on its springs. He circled around the front of the vehicle and opened the smaller pedestrian gate. "Where to now?" He asked.

"Down this set of stairs, then when we get to the pool deck go down four or five more steps and turn right, into the garden. The pile of mush is just over the edge of the pool deck."

"Okay." He said, clambering down the wide stairs towards the main level of the large house. "Pretty fancy place for just one person to rent."

"It is excessive. And she wears cheap clothes."

"Again, with the cheap clothes. What's the deal?"

"It's inconsistent."

"Okay. I'll give you that."

Jessica pointed, "There's the stuff Sparky was interested in."

Ramirez squatted near the pile of soggy vegetation. He picked up a small branch that had fallen off a nearby shrub and carefully prodded the odorous heap. "I don't want to touch this in case it is the source of the poison."

"No kidding, I'm not going near it. I feel badly that Sparky was close enough to give it a sniff."

"Definitely looks like it has been cooked, and for quite a long time." He said.

Ramirez reached into his pocket for a plastic evidence bag and with a slight grimace stuck his hand inside as if he was a pet owner about to pick up a pile of hot, fresh dog poop. "Okay, that should do it," He said, tying a knot in the top of the bag. "Let's go back to the station."

Chapter 45

February 8th Isla Mujeres

"We need to get this tested as quickly as possible," Ramirez said, holding up the clear plastic evidence bag.

"I'll take it," Cervera held out his hand, "we can get that done faster in Cancun."

"Wouldn't someone familiar with plants, especially poisonous plants that grow on the island be able to identify the leaves and tell us whether or not it might be the source of the poison?" Asked Jessica.

"What do you think Ramirez?" Cervera asked, aiming the question over his shoulder while he studied Jessica.

"Worth a try," Ramirez still held the bag of vegetation in his hand.

Cervera jerked his head in agreement, "Does anyone know a plant expert on the island?"

"How about Doctora Marion?" Jessica answered before anyone else had a chance to utter a syllable. "She has probably seen her share of curious toddlers tasting toxic plants."

Ramirez considered that for a moment, then nodded in agreement, "Constable Gomez, run this over to the doctora's clinic and see what she thinks," He said, handing the bag to Alexis.

"Should I stop by the rental house to pick up the big pot from Luz, the one that she thinks was recently used to boil something?" Alexis asked.

"Good thinking," Ramirez agreed. "I should have done that when Jessica and I were there a few minutes ago."

Watching Alexis hustle out the door with a junior constable in her wake, Ramirez said to Cervera, "We need to have a chat with our guests, plus I'm still holding the captain, Damien Hau."

"Who do you want to start with?" Cervera asked.

"How about we talk to Hau while we wait to see if the doctora can identify the plant?"

"Sounds good, then we can deal with Bruno Torres and leave the delightful señora to the last." Cervera said, smiling broadly at Toledo and Ramirez.

"Anyone know where Sargent Ramirez is?" Alexis asked, her face was pink with excitement.

Jessica yawned and pointed towards the interview room, "in there. Can you ask Felipe if we are free to leave? Mike and I are dead tired from all this waiting around, and Sparky needs a pee break."

Alexis nodded, and lightly rapped on the door then waited for Ramirez to answer.

"Did you get confirmation?" Ramirez asked.

"Yes, Doctora Marion is quite certain these are leaves from an Angels' Trumpet part of the Brugmansia plant family and they are highly toxic." She said, her eyes shining with eagerness. "And I got the pot, too."

"Good work, Alexis," Ramirez said.

"Jessica and Mike want to leave. Is that okay?"

"Sure, but they'll miss all the fun if they leave," He said with a sly smile. "While you were at the doctora's we searched the señora's luggage. It turns out she has two passports under different names and one is similar to the dead guy's last name: Suzanne Hamilton-Forbes."

"Madre de Dios," Alexis whispered, "she's his wife."

"Possibly, Cervera is interviewing her now."

In the interview room Cervera gave the two chairs that were on the interviewer's side of the table a searching look. Perhaps an angry detainee had attempted to battle his way past the arresting officers. The leg on one was twisted at an odd angle, and it rocked alarmingly when he gave it an exploratory jiggle. The other chair had a twisted seat, and one bent leg.

Cervera gingerly lowered his bulk onto the least damaged chair, leaving the other for Toledo; payback for his caustic remarks about Cervera's weight.

"Señora Suzanne Hamilton-Forbes, I am Detective Cervera of the State Police, and this is my partner Detective Toledo," He said, "And I believe that you are already acquainted with Sergeant Ramirez of the Municipal Police," He said indicating the figure leaning against the door frame.

271

"My name is Sophia Hayden-Smith," The woman snapped. "Take these handcuffs off me, now!" She held out her wrists.

"No need to be rude, señora," Cervera said mildly. "You've been legally detained and until we are satisfied with your explanations, you must remain handcuffed."

"You have the wrong person. I am Sophia Hayden-Smith," She emphasised.

"Mm, perhaps, but oddly the photographs in both of these passports look like you," He placed the two American passports on the metal desk. "Could you explain that to us, please?"

Suzanne drew her lips back in a weasel-like snarl, "I want a lawyer."

"Of course, as you wish," Cervera agreed amicably, "But you might want to rethink that."

"I demand to see a lawyer."

"Lawyers in Mexico handle minor legal problems," He said, "The notarios are the ones who handle criminal cases."

"Whatever! I am not speaking to you without legal representation."

"That's fine, señora. Shall we contact a local notario for you, or do you wish to wait for your own to come from Nashville?"

"My lawyer, from Nashville, I am not trusting my freedom to some local bozo with an on-line certificate stating he knows how to fight parking tickets," She retorted. "Now release me. I will stay in a hotel in Cancun, and you can hold my passport."

Cervera sighed, and shook his head, "señora Hamilton-Forbes you are under arrest for the murder of your husband Brandon Forbes. You will remain as our guest until your trial." He pinned her with his dark eyes, "Now do you understand the seriousness of your situation?"

"I'll pay," Hamilton-Forbes stated, her eyes calmly clocking each man in turn. Cervera, then Toledo, then Ramirez. "All of you, how much?"

Startled at the sudden switch from demanding a lawyer, to offering a bribe, Cervera forgot the deplorable condition of the chair that he was perched on and leaned back. He felt the chair rock alarmingly with the shift of his weight and quickly righted himself. "Perdón señora? Are you offering us a bribe to release you?" He asked.

"Of course. Money solves all problems," She said confidently, "How much?"

"Bribing a police officer is a crime. Accepting a bribe could also land the three of us in jail alongside you."

"Let's cut to the chase," She laughed, and leaned forward, "My best offer is the equivalent of one year's wages, for each of you," She said, confidentially.

Cervera met Toledo's eyes, and raised his eyebrows in a question. Toledo twitched his head: *no*. Next his eyes settled on Ramirez, with the same unspoken question; *do you?* Ramirez appeared uncertain as he reluctantly signalled: *no*.

"I'm sorry señora, it appears that you don't have any takers on your offer."

"Take your time and think it over," She said to Cervera, "You have until my legal representative arrives to make your decision." Her calculating grin reminded Cervera of a crocodile, particularly the one that lived at the Hacienda Mundaca. "If you aren't interested, I'm certain the man in charge of this …" she fluttered her hand to indicate the police station, "… dump, would be. Now, take me back to that hell hole you call a holding cell."

Ramirez grasped her bicep, guiding her towards the door. As he exited the room, he gave Cervera a quiet look that could have said; *don't you dare make a deal*. Or it could have said; *maybe we should*.

Cervera leaned his chin on the palm of his hand. This was interesting. He'd been offered bribes before, but never an entire year's wages.

Ramirez re-entered the room, locked the door, and sat in the third chair, "Are you tempted?" He asked Cervera.

Cervera held up his cell phone and deliberately turned it off, motioning to the other two to do the same, then he nodded, "Si, very tempted. I'm closer to retirement than either of you. But sadly, I'm going to turn her down. I have no desire to spend my golden years in a cell."

"Toledo? What about you?" Ramirez asked.

"Tempted, absolutely. But, no thanks," He answered, "Spending time in prison with people that we put away doesn't fit with my plans either."

"What about you, Ramirez?" Cervera asked.

Ramirez held his thumb and forefinger close together, "This close to saying yes," He sighed. "Unfortunately, even if we say no, the comandante will likely say yes."

Chapter 46

February 9th Isla Mujeres

Jessica sat on the edge of the pathway at Punta Sur, with Sparky at her feet, exactly where she had been when she first met Mike Lyons several months ago.

This time Mike's comfortable bulk was beside her, his arm around her shoulders and his other hand lightly scratching Sparky's ears. The multi-toned blues of the Caribbean Sea sparkled beneath the rising sun and a gentle surf rolled over the rocky shore, expiring against the cliff.

Paradise. Her paradise.

"It's really sad the Friday night event ended the way it did," Mike said.

"No kidding. It was the one night that I was really looking forward to then that stupid woman decided to kill her husband," Jessica said. "Did you go to the wind-up event at *Kin Há* yesterday?"

Mike leaned closer and kissed the top of her head, "No, I wasn't in the mood, and I really wanted to go with you, not by myself."

"I'm sorry about that, Mike, but I was scheduled to work again."

"Don't worry about it."

"Well, at least none of my friends were in danger this time, and Sparky and I survived unscathed," She said, tilting her head so that she could absorb the kindness in Mike's eyes.

He smiled and brushed her lips with his, "Mmm, and I'm very happy you are still in one piece."

"And, I'm relieved that no one I know was shot, kidnapped, or stabbed," She lifted a palm to rest it lightly against his short beard.

"Sergeant Ramirez warned me about how dangerous it was to be around you," He mumbled into her lips.

Returning his kiss, her mouth tweaked up on one side as she recalled the incident, "Felipe can be a pain in the ass."

"I got that impression from the look that you exchanged with Alexis," Mike leaned back, a teasing smile creased his face and crinkled the corners of his eyes.

"He likes to needle me by mimicking Comandante Camara," She made a face. "Their boss detests me and he has great hopes that some day soon, I will vanish forever from his life," She said. "Did you also know that the comandante says I am responsible for the increase of the island's crime rate?"

"How?"

"According to him, I attract trouble. The murderers and hitmen are drawn to me like a moth to a porchlight."

"Flame," Mike corrected, "like a moth to a flame."

"Nun-uh. He said porchlight," She smiled, "You would've been impressed. I refrained from correcting him."

"Well done," Mike said, "speaking of the policía, Ramirez told me that Suzanne Hamilton-Forbes was allowed to leave Mexico and fly her personal jet back to Nashville."

Jessica straightened up, "Are you kidding me?" She asked, her tone pitched with sarcastic astonishment.

"Afraid not," He said, "according to Ramirez, she was released on her own recognisance and instructed to return at a later date for the trial."

"Un-freaking-believable," Jessica snorted.

"Well, it's not our problem," He said.

"No, it's not, but what about the other guy, Torres?" She asked, "Did he have a get out of jail free card too?"

"I don't know. I didn't think to ask."

She waved away the comment, "He probably didn't have enough dinero."

"Maybe," Mike quietly agreed, "Jess … have you ever thought about leaving Isla?" He stumbled uncertainly, "Trying something different?"

She mulled that over for a moment, "Yeah, sometimes. I get antsy for a new adventure, but I really enjoy Isla."

"Me too, but unfortunately I need to earn a living," He said, turning to look in her eyes. "Jess, I'm leaving soon."

"Oh? Are you headed back to Canada?" Jessica felt her heart cramp at the thought of Mike leaving the island. In the past few weeks, she had grown tremendously fond of him.

"No, I've signed a new contract with *The Mighty Yee* winery in California. The owner wants me to do a check of their procedures to see if I can streamline her production."

Leaning back, distancing herself, "*The Mighty Yee*, what a great name," She said, hoping she didn't sound as sulky and disappointed as she felt.

"It fits perfectly. Linda Yee is a petit bundle of extraordinary vitality and contagious enthusiasm," Mike said. "I'm really looking forward to working with her."

"It sounds like it will be a fun adventure." Mike's eagerness to work with the female winery owner caused a frisson of jealousy to skitter over Jessica's skin. She had no claim on him, but still ... he could at least pretend he would miss her.

Mike reached again for Jessica's hand, and smiled into her eyes, "I was wondering if you would like to come with me?" He asked, gently rubbing his thumb over her palm.

"Oh," Jessica stilled for a moment then carefully extracted her hand from his. She leaned over to hug her pooch, "I don't know, Mike, what would I do with Sparky?" Her mind raced with the implications of his question. *Did she want to go with him? She hardly knew him yet she was strongly attracted to him.*

"He's allowed to come with you."

"You mean he's allowed to enter the USA with proper documentation," She said, amending his statement, "I know personal pets can be transported between Mexico, the USA, and Canada assuming they have had the necessary shots and have a recent certificate of health." *Jesus. Why was she nervously motor-mouthing about certificates of health and documentation?*

Mike swept the flat of his hand down his face, and then held his palm partially covering his mouth and chin. He peered sheepishly at Jessica, "Um, no, I meant you can bring him to the winery with you. I asked."

"You asked?" Jessica queried, "Who, the owner Linda Yee?"

He nervously scrubbed his hand over his balding head, "Yeah, I asked her if Sparky and you could come with me ... just in case ... you said yes."

She stiffened and shifted away from Mike. "So, this isn't a spur-of-the-moment question? You've been planning this?"

"Jess, I have been stewing over this for weeks, please don't be upset at me."

"Well ... no ... I'm not upset. I'm surprised, that's all. I'm not accustomed to someone else organizing my life," She said. "Besides, what would I do for work? I have to support myself. And where would I live?"

"Ah hell, you are going to think I'm a complete control freak," Mike temporised. "The contract can be amended to add you as my winery assistant and the winery owns a guest cottage that will be available for us to use," He hastened to add, "but it has two ensuite bedrooms both with locking doors, so you can have your privacy … if you want it."

Mike held palms up, capitulating, "I know, too much all at once. I'm really sorry if I've made you uncomfortable, but I wanted to know if this was doable before I asked you to come with me."

He sheepishly smiled, "I'm babbling. I'll just shut up now."

"When do you need to know?" She saw his shoulders sag with what looked like disappointment when she asked another question instead of answering his.

"I start work in a week."

Trying to sound as if she was clarifying and not criticizing, Jessica said, "If I say yes, that's not much time to wrap up my life here."

"I know, my fault. I was too chicken to ask you sooner."

"Chicken?" Now, she was truly perplexed, "Why?"

"I'm terrified you'll say no," Mike looked at her, his face reflecting his uncertainty and his longing.

Wrapping her arms defensively across her body she looked out over the ocean, "I'm not sure, Mike. I need a day or two to think about this."

Chapter 47

February 9th Isla Mujeres

Twirling the stem of her wine glass, Jessica watched the red liquid rise and fall like a tiny whirlpool. "What do you think, Yassy?" She had just finished recounting her sunrise conversation with Mike.

"Do you love him?" Yasmin asked.

Jessica looked at her closest friend, and knew she couldn't answer that simple question with certainty. "That's my problem," She said, "I think I love him, but we have only known each other a short time."

She fiddled with her glass then took a sip of wine, and grinned at Yasmin, "Despite my obvious enjoyment of recreational sex," She comically bounced her eyebrows, "I actually believe a durable love develops slowly from a strong friendship. It doesn't just burst into being with a flash of lust," She said imitating a burst of fireworks with her fingers.

"I totally agree," Yasmin said. "So, is he fun in bed?"

Jessica's face pinked, "I don't actually know."

"Are you kidding me?" Yasmin asked, gripping Jessica's wrist and giving it a little shake. "You haven't had sex with him yet?"

"No, it just hasn't happened."

"How will you know if you are compatible if you don't do the *cuchi-cuchi*?"

"Leaving Isla doesn't have to be permanent. I can afford to keep my place for a month or two before I decide," She said, waving her hand, indicating her little rental house and her belongings.

"Like an escape plan, then?"

"Sort of," She squirmed, dropping her eyes away from Yasmin's calculating stare. "More like a back-up plan in case things don't … you know … work out."

"But you do like him?" Yasmin probed.

"Yes, I do," Jessica raised her eyes to meet Yasmin's. "He's kind, and cheerful, and down-to-earth. He has a wacky sense of humour that I totally get," Her eyes crinkled with mirth. "Did I tell you his goofy diagnosis of my golf cart problem? He said it as a broken chrome-reverse-sliding-gear."

"Si. That was funny, and quick witted."

"His humour is a big part of why I'm attracted to him," Jessica said. "What would you do, Yassy?"

"Jess, I am so not you. I'm not an adventurer," Yasmin said, placing her hand lightly on Jessica's forearm, "I love my island, my culture, and I'm deeply in love with Carlos. Having our families nearby is very important to both Carlos and me. I couldn't leave everything to travel the world."

"Damn, you're no help at all," Jessica moaned. "I'm no closer to making a decision than I was an hour ago, and we've polished off my only bottle of wine," She waggled the empty bottle back and forth before getting up to toss it into the garbage can.

"Sorry mi amiga, this decision is all yours," Yasmin said, "We love you and if you decide to go with Mike, you'll always be a part of our lives."

"Great, now I'm crying," Jessica sniffed back a slimy laugh. "I'll need a big hunk of paper towel to clean up this mess," She said. Reaching for the roll of Bounty she unwound a few sections, balled it up in her hand and loudly honked into it.

"Me too," Yasmin laughed as she reached for the same roll.

"3:00 in the bloody morning and I'm still wide awake," Jessica moaned, then smashed her pillow over her head.

She heard a soft thumping sound from the floor of her bedroom, "Am I keeping you awake, Sparky?" She mumbled.

At the sound of her voice the thumping increased in tempo. "Yep, you're awake too," She extracted her head from under the pillow and tossed off the covers.

His tail swishing happily, Sparky bowed in a full-body stretch then placed his front paws on her knees. Wrapping him in a hug she vigorously scratched his ears and then his rump. "Who's a good boy?" She asked her grinning pooch.

She picked up her phone and keyed in one word, "Yes," then headed to the kitchen and turned on the coffee maker.

Four minutes later her phone beeped with an incoming call.

"I'm a very happy man," Said a sleepy voice.

El Fin

But wait, there's more...

Follow Sparky, Jessica, and Mike in their new adventures: The Wine Country Mystery series. Coming early in 2021!

About the author

Born in a British Columbia Canada gold mining community that is now essentially a ghost town, Lynda has had a very diverse, some might say eccentric, working career. Her employment background has included a bank clerk, antique store owner, ambulance attendant, volunteer firefighter, supervisor of the SkyTrain transit control centre, partner in a bed & breakfast, partner in a microbrewery, and a hotel manager. The adventure and the experience were always far more important than the paycheque.

Writing has always been in the background of her life, starting with travel articles for a local newspaper, an unpublished novel written before her fortieth birthday, and articles for an American safety magazine.

When she and her husband, Lawrie Lock, retired to Isla Mujeres, Mexico in 2008, they started a weekly blog, Notes from Paradise, to keep friends and family up to date on their newest adventure.

Needing something more to keep her active mind occupied, Lynda and island friend, Diego Medina, self-published a bi-lingual book for children, The Adventures of Thomas the Cat / Las Aventuras de Tómas el Gato. The book won Silver at the 2016 International Latino Book Awards for best bi-lingual picture book for children.

Well, one thing led to another and here we have the Isla Mujeres Mystery series, set on an island in the Caribbean Sea near Cancun Mexico.

The legal stuff

The characters and events in this book are purely fictional except the following:

Jessica Sanderson is a product of my imagination but like me, she was born in BC Canada. She shares my off-beat sense of humour, potty mouth, and a love of critters.

Carlos Mendoza is in many ways my husband Lawrie Lock. He has his good sense of humour, the love of dancing, plus the appreciation of Rolex watches and expensive cars. Lawrie and his three life-long buddies Don, Erle, and Duke managed to get into a few interesting situations when they were younger.

Yasmin Medina is completely fictitious, but she is tall with curly hair similar to my friend Yazmin Aguirre.

The *Loco Lobo Restaurant* is fictitious, it is not based on any particular location or restaurant.

The Island Time Music Fest is real. The coordinators graciously allowed me to use their event as the backdrop for this novel. They are not responsible for any of the shenanigans that my characters got up to during their annual fundraising event.

Big Daddy's on the Beach is also real. The owners graciously allowed me to use their restaurant in Twisted Isla. They are definitely not responsible for any of the high jinks that my characters were involved in on the premises.

Twisted Isla
Published by Lynda L. Lock
Copyright 2020
Print Copy: ISBN 978 1 775 3788 8 4
Electronic Book: ISBN 978 1 775 3788 7 7

Hola amigos y amigas

Pardon my lack of Spanish. I keep trying to learn, but every night while I am sleeping the words leak out of my brain and onto the pillow.

In a perfect world I would have written this story in Spanish or in this case Isla-Spanish which is a colourful mix of local expressions and a bit of Mayan tossed in for added flavour.

However, most of my readers are English speaking. So, for the purpose of this story the local folks are fluent in both Spanish and English, especially the cuss words.

I chose to *italicise* only a few of the less familiar Spanish expressions. For my American fans you will probably notice I spell some words differently. The British-Canadian spelling that I grew up with is what I use.

Like every self-published writer, I rely heavily on recommendations and reviews to sell my books. If you enjoyed reading any of my *Isla Mujeres Mystery* novels please leave a review on Amazon, Goodreads, Bookbub, Facebook or Twitter. Tell your friends, tell your family, or anyone who will listen. Word-of-mouth is enormously helpful.

If you come across an annoying blunder please email me at: lock.lynda@gmail.com and I will make it disappear.

You can also find Sparky and me on social media:
A Writer's Life
Facebook @ Lynda L Lock
Twitter @ Isla Mysteries
Instagram @ Isla Mysteries
Amazon @ Lynda L Lock
Bookbub @ Lynda L Lock
Goodreads @ Lynda L Lock

Like this book? Please try the others!

Buy all 5 books with one click

Acknowledgements

Writing is a solitary obsession with hours spent creating, considering, and correcting.

However, I have had assistance from some amazing people:

- Captain Tony Garcia for the beautiful cover photos for the first three novels plus the photo of Sparky and me. He is also a valuable source of information about island life.
- You may have guessed by now Tony Garcia and Betsy Snider are good friends. They are owned by several yellow cats, and two dogs. Kitty-Kitty a pale-orange love-bug, is their favourite.
- Carmen Amato, mystery writer and creator of the Emilia Cruz Detective Series re-designed the covers for both *Treasure Isla* and *Trouble Isla*.
- Our good friends Diego Medina and Jeff McGahee patiently tweaked the cover for *Tormenta Isla* until I was happy with the results.
- Diego Medina created the covers for Temptation Isla, Terror Isla, Twisted Isla from some of my photos.
- Patricio Yam Dzul, Aida Yolanda Pérez Martín, Freddy Medina and Eva Velázquez are cherished friends who are always willing to share their life stories.
- Apache (Isauro Martinez Jr.) another one of my go-to-friends when I am searching for specific information about the island.
- Julie and Rob Goth for Island Time Music Fest details.
- The recording sunglasses were a Christmas gift from my fun-loving husband, Lawrie Lock.
- The chrome-reverse-sliding gear assessment was a Lawrie-ism that won my heart.
- Manuscript and proofreaders include, Rob Goth, Julie Andrews Goth, Sue Lo, Betsy Snider, Janice Carlisle Rodgers, John Cargill, and Karen Cargill.

I truly appreciate your helpful suggestions and corrections, any and all remaining errors are my responsibility.

- A special thanks to Sue Lo who did the final proofing, and found a way at the end of the book for Sparky to get his mojo back. He had been feeling glum because he hadn't recently solved a crime.

There are four other groups of people I would like to thank for their continuing encouragement and support:

- Faithful readers of Notes from Paradise – A Writer's Life
- Supporters of my children's book, The Adventures of Thomas the Cat;
- Fans of the Isla Mujeres Mystery series;
- And our island friends, expats and born-here-locals who patiently answered my questions about this and that and everything.

Thank you, thank you, and thank you all!

Neighbours helping neighbours:

If you wish to help your fellow islanders during the health and economic crisis created by the COVID19 pandemic, here are a few suggestions from the folks on the ground who are battling against the hunger and the uncertainty.

Feed Isla: A very active group of concerned locals, plus resident and non-resident foreigners, who are partnered with local organizations and businesses to provide nutritious meals and basic necessities for islanders. The group has also distributed thousands of Chedraui grocery store gift cards and/or pantries containing basic foodstuffs.

https://www.facebook.com/feedisla/ PayPal - feedisla@gmail.com

Rosa Sirena's Restaurant & Rooftop Palapa Bar:

Deborah Crinigan de Chacón plus chefs Willy Chacón, Victor Montañez Chan and Salomon Gurubel, providing thousands of hot meals for Isla families.

https://www.facebook.com/rosasirenasrestaurant/

The Joint Reggae Bar:

Penny Demming and The Joint's staff preparing and distributing meals.

https://www.facebook.com/thejointislamujeres/

Brenda's Isla Angels Savannah's Pantry:

Brenda Nash Lamonica, providing baby diapers, wipes, formulas, milk and some baby food.

https://paypal.me/savannahspantry?locale.x=en_US

https://www.facebook.com/113392477064858/posts/114854330252006/

Asia Caribe: Annelise & Peter Krinisky meals for families.

https://www.facebook.com/AsiaCaribeIsla/

Diana Martinez: Isla Mujeres Scholarship Program's student Diana Martinez feeding approximately 150 vulnerable families daily.

PayPal - moongrl722@gmail.com

Javi's Cantina: Javier Martinez and Marla Bainbridge Martinez. Making and delivering hot meals for needy islanders.

https://www.facebook.com/javiscantina/

Ruben Chavez Martinez: Feeding families and providing the basics. Assisting seniors with paying electric bills and purchasing medications. PayPal - https://www.paypal.me/RubenChavezM

Rescuing the Islanders: Sergio Ventura and team Feeding families and providing other necessities.

PayPal serchtec20@gmail.com

https://www.facebook.com/groups/218078596144332/?ref=share

Friends of Keys 4 Life: Ken and Debbie Wanovich. Providing food and other necessities

https://www.keys4life.org/

Isla Diabetes Clinic: Purchase needed Personal Protective Equipment (PPE) for Isla's frontline medical workers.

PayPal isladiabetesclinic@gmail.com
https://www.facebook.com/isladiabetesclinic/

Thank you to some of the delivery teams:

Fabian Rebolledo & Clara Yam (Guadalupana);

Annie Contreras (Isla Lashes) & Roberto Smith (Isla Driver Robby);

Twisted Isla

Tommy & Allison Merandi (BIO GREEN BLUE);

Jeff & Rhett McGahee (Isla Brewing Company - Cerveza Isla);

Chris Lane (Mundaca Real Estate) (IslaMujeres.info),

Mati Ross and Crystal Steele.

Helping the four-legged islanders:

Helping Animals Living Overseas: Clinica Veterinaria, Drs. Delfino Guevara, Rossely Gonzalez, Anna Gabriela Flores

https://www.facebook.com/clinicavetim/
https://www.helpinganimalslivingoverseas.org

Isla Cats: Josefina Rodriguez Martinez - PayPal islacats.food.help@gmail.com

Isla Animals: http://www.islaanimals.org

http://islaanimals.org/donate-animal-rescue-isla-animals/

Pet Food Project:
https://www.facebook.com/groups/petfoodproject/?hc_location=group

For readers who are a little Spanish-challenged

Bruja del Mar – Literally witch of the sea, Sea Witch
Carina – urban slang for a funny, gorgeous, and amazing girlfriend
Casita – small house
Casa – house
Claro or claro que sí – agreement, of course
Cómo está? – How are you?
Con permiso – to move around or past a person
Cuchi-cuchi – humorous euphemism for sex
Don or Doña – respectful title used with the person's first name
Hermano – brother, or any male who is like a brother
Hermana – sister, or any female who is like a sister
Hijo de la chingada – crude curse, son of a bitch
Hola – hi or hello
Hombre – man
La Trigueña – The young woman Mundaca loved
Loco Lobo – Crazy Wolf, also El Loco Lobo but one of our Mexican friends said Loco Lobo sounded better
Maldito – darn, damn
Mama - mom
Mami – mommy
Mande? – The person didn't hear you.
Más o menos – more or less
Mi amor – my love
Mierda – swear word, shit
Mordidita – bribe, literally a little bite
Motos – motor scooters, motor bikes
Niña(s) – girl or girls
Niño(s) – boy or boys, can also mean children
Papa - dad
Papi – daddy
Pendejo – swear word
Que pasa – what's happening
Que pasó – what happened
Pícaro – horndog, randy male
Rapido – rapid, fast

Twisted Isla

Testamentos – wills
Tia – auntie, or an older female who is like an aunt
Tio – uncle, or an older male who is like an uncle
Topes – speed bumps

Sparky and his writer

Manufactured by Amazon.ca
Bolton, ON